Family Story Collection

⌘ VOLUME 2 ⌘

75 More Fables for Living, Loving, & Learning

INCLUDING STORIES FROM YOUR FAVORITE DISNEY·PIXAR FILMS

Disney

Family Story Collection

~ VOLUME 2 ~

75 More Fables for Living, Loving, & Learning

Foreword by the Reverend Michael Catlett

Adapted by Catherine Hapka, Emily Neye, and Laura Driscoll
Jacket illustration by Dick Kelsey and Ron Dias

INCLUDING STORIES FROM YOUR FAVORITE Disney·PIXAR FILMS

Disney
PRESS

NEW YORK

Contents

Foreword

My daughter Ruth was four years old when the original *Disney's Family Story Collection* was first printed. Back then, she listened to stories that were read to her. She hung on to every word as the characters came to life—sometimes overwhelming her. She was more of an observer than a participant with these stories.

Now she is eight. She can read the stories by herself, bravely sounding out words and trying out new thoughts and ideas to see if they fit. Sometimes she reads aloud and our family has the chance to hear the story, along with her own commentary. She has that jack-o'-lantern look to her, a gap-toothed smile that offers irrefutable evidence that her baby years will soon be over and her teen years have begun their inevitable arrival.

As she and the rest of our children make the transition from toddler to teen, from little girl to young woman, from small boy to young man, from a handful to a heart full, I hope they will continue to find that the Disney stories offer a wonderful perspective on life. There is much we all can learn from these stories if we continue to listen with our imagination and creativity to the truths that resonate within them.

In this book, Tarzan reminds us that love and compassion define a family, not appearance or birth. In *Monsters, Inc.*, Sulley and Mike discover that laughter is more powerful than fear—a chuckle of greater value than a scream.

Buzz and Woody, in *Toy Story 2*, show us that working together accomplishes far more than working alone. In *102 Dalmatians*, Oddball knows what it is like to be different yet discovers that being unique is also a reason to rejoice. And Milo, in *Atlantis: The Lost Empire,* understands that a dream can propel us to new places and enable us to make discoveries about others and ourselves.

This book is a collection of hopes and dreams drawn and written for children of all ages. Open the pages and for a few moments become a child again. Look at the pictures, listen to the tales, and discover once more the power of a story well told. Open your heart to Milo's courage and Sulley's laugh. Open your arms to a child and listen for the truths they find as they read and hear the stories. Learn what most every gap-toothed child knows—that wisdom does not reside in simple statements but lives forever in wonderful stories.

Michael Catlett
Pastor, McLean Baptist Church

YOU CAN COUNT ON ME

STORIES ABOUT FAMILY, LOVE, AND FRIENDSHIP

Tigger Finds a Family

from *The Tigger Movie*

Sometimes the love you're looking for is right under your whiskers.

ormally Tigger would sing, "The most wonderful thing about tiggers is I'm the only one!" Today, however, being the only one was making him feel lonely, not wonderful. Roo saw how sad Tigger was and tried to comfort him. Maybe there *were* other tiggers out there, Roo suggested. Roo had his mother, Kanga, so why shouldn't Tigger have a family, too?

"Can you imaginate it?" he asked Roo. "There'd be more tiggers than you could shake a stick at! And we'd all be bouncin'!"

Tigger and Roo wandered all through the woods, calling out, "Halloo! Tigger family!" but they had no luck.

So, they decided to write a letter to the other tiggers of the world. They put the letter in the mail and anxiously awaited a reply.

It didn't take long before Tigger got discouraged. "Why am I kiddin' myself?" he said. "I might as well face it. There aren't any other tiggers."

All the friends gathered together the next day. They hated to see Tigger so upset. Then Owl had an idea. "Young Roo," he said, "if you suggest that a letter will bring cheer to our friend Tigger, then we shall, by all means, write one."

It was easy to pretend to be Tigger's family because everyone loved him so much. "Dress warmly," wrote Kanga. "Eat well," added Pooh. "Stay safe and sound, and keep smiling," wrote Piglet and Eeyore. And finally, Roo closed the letter with, "We're always there for you."

The next morning, when Tigger received the letter, he was as happy as could be. But there was one problem: Tigger thought that his family was going to visit him the very next day. The friends knew they had to tell Tigger that they had written the letter, but nobody had the heart to break the bad news.

Instead, they dressed up like tiggers and showed up at Tigger's house. Tigger wasn't fooled for long. When he realized what they had done, he felt

lonelier than ever. He went off into the woods by himself and climbed up into a tall tree.

He read his letter over and over. "But . . . I thought you were always there for me," he said to himself, as the letter slipped through his hands and blew away.

A little while later, Tigger heard his name being called. He looked down in surprise. At first he thought his tigger family had finally arrived, but then he saw it was just his old friends—Owl, Kanga, Pooh, Piglet, Eeyore, Rabbit, and Roo. Tigger was so focused on seeing tiggers that he didn't see the family that was right before his eyes.

Tigger and his friends all went back home together, but Tigger still seemed sad. He wished he hadn't lost his letter, because he had begun to forget what it said. Then his friends recited the words they had written.

"You mean *you* fellas are my family? I shoulda seen it all along!" said Tigger. Tigger was so happy, he decided to give each member of his "family" a gift. And he gave an extra-special gift to Roo: it was a locket he had been waiting to fill with a family portrait. But he didn't have to wait any longer. He placed a picture of all his friends inside.

Set Free

from *Beauty and the Beast*

True love means putting another's happiness above your own.

The Beast desperately wanted to break the spell that had turned him into a monster and his servants into enchanted objects. But he had only a short time left to learn to love someone, and to earn her love in return.

The servants thought that Belle could be the answer. The Beast had taken her prisoner, but lately the two had become friends.

As he watched Belle enjoying a snowy day in the castle yard, the Beast sighed. "I've never felt this way about anyone," he told his servants. "I want to do something for her. But what?"

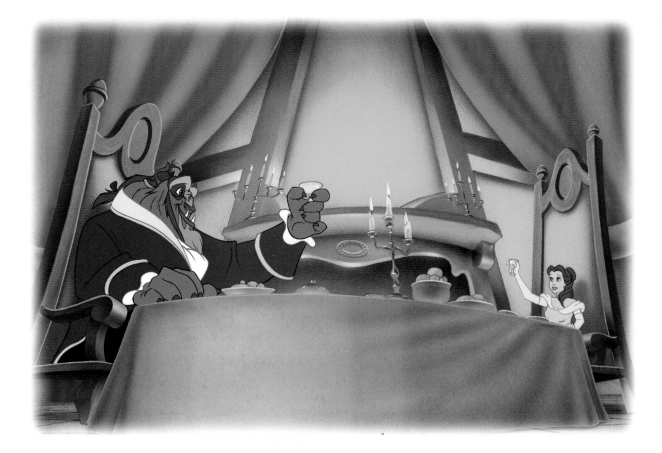

Lumiere, the candelabrum, gave him the perfect idea. Later, the Beast led Belle into a hallway and told her to close her eyes.

She did. She trusted the Beast. He took her into a glorious library, with books stacked from floor to ceiling. Belle gasped. She loved reading—it was the perfect gift!

They all hoped Belle would be the one to break the spell. To help things along, they arranged a special evening for the pair. Belle and the Beast dressed up in their finest clothes and met for a beautiful evening of dinner and dancing.

Afterward, they sat on the terrace under a canopy of stars. "Belle," the Beast asked softly, "are you happy here with me?"

"Yes!" she responded instantly. But then her face grew sad, and she glanced away.

"What is it?" the Beast asked.

"If only I could see my father again—just for a moment," Belle said. "I miss him so much."

The Beast had an idea. "There is a way. . . ."

He handed her a magic mirror. It would show her anything she wanted to see. Belle asked to see her father.

When he appeared in the mirror, he was coughing and struggling through deep snow. "Papa! Oh, no!" Belle cried. "He's sick—and he's all alone!"

The Beast could feel her pain as if it were his own. "Then you must go to him," he said. "I release you. You're no longer my prisoner."

"You mean—I'm free?" Belle was amazed. "Oh, thank you! Hold on, Papa! I'm on my way!"

As she rushed out of the room, Cogsworth, the mantel clock, entered.

"I let her go," the Beast told him.

"You what?" Cogsworth exclaimed in dismay. "How could you do that?"

"I had to." The Beast gazed after Belle. "I love her."

The Beast had finally learned to love another. In doing so, he had realized something important— keeping Belle a prisoner would not force her to love him in return. And he would rather see her happy than keep her against her will—even if it meant he was doomed to remain a beast forever.

In My Heart

from *Tarzan*®

Family is more than skin-deep.

Kala was heartbroken when the leopard, Sabor, took her little gorilla. So, when she heard a baby's cry in the jungle, she had to follow it, though she knew it couldn't possibly be her lost little one.

To her surprise, the baby she found had pink skin and only a tiny bit of fur on the top of its head. Still, it was so helpless and small that Kala couldn't resist picking it up.

It didn't take long for Kala to take young Tarzan into her heart as
her own child. Some of the other apes, however, were not so quick to
accept him. Most of the younger apes made fun of the strange
youngster, and Kerchak, the leader of the ape family, didn't trust him.
Tarzan was so different, with his smooth skin and odd appearance.
How could he ever be one of them?

Even Tarzan's best friend, Terk, was embarrassed to be seen with
him. "Personally, I'd love to hang out with you," she told him. "But
the guys, they need a little convincing."

Tarzan tried his hardest to convince the other apes to accept him.
But no matter what he did, it didn't work. He was just too different.

When Tarzan accidentally caused an elephant stampede, Kerchak got fed up with him. "You'll never learn!" the ape leader raged. "You can't learn to be one of us! You'll never fit into this family!"

Kala started to argue with Kerchak, but Tarzan didn't stick around to hear it. He ran away from camp.

A few minutes later, he stared at his own reflection in the water. His pale, hairless face stared back at him. Why did he have to be so different? Why couldn't he fit in?

He smeared mud on his face and arms, trying to look more like an ape. Kala found him staring at his new reflection.

"Never mind what Kerchak said," she told him gently, wiping away the mud.

"But look at me!" Tarzan cried.

"I am," she told him. "And do you know what I see? I see two eyes, like mine. Two ears . . . and let's see, what else?"

"Two hands?" Tarzan guessed. He put his small hands against her large ones. They looked very different. But Kala explained that it didn't matter, because their hearts were the same.

That made Tarzan feel much better. He still wasn't sure if he would ever fit in with the other apes. But it was nice to know that Kala—his mother—accepted him just as he was.

'Ohana Means Family

from *Lilo & Stitch*

Family means nobody gets left behind or forgotten.

Lilo was lonely. Her older sister, Nani, worked all the time. Sometimes she felt as though her only friend was Pudge the fish—and he probably only liked her for the sandwiches she brought him.

Sometimes Lilo got so lonely and sad that she believed she didn't belong anywhere. One day, Nani was late picking her up from hula

class. Lilo ran home, locked herself in the house, and turned on her record player. She lay on the floor, wondering if anyone would ever care about her again.

Nani rushed home to find her. "Open the door, Lilo!" she called through the dog door. "We don't have time for this! The social worker's going to be here any minute!"

But Lilo didn't listen, and the social worker wound up scolding Nani for leaving Lilo home alone. After he had left, Nani yelled at Lilo. "Why didn't you wait at the school? Do you want to be taken away? Answer me!"

"No!" Lilo yelled back. "Why don't you sell me and buy a rabbit instead?"

Later, Nani came into Lilo's room. "We're a broken family, aren't we?" Lilo asked her sadly.

"Maybe a little," Nani admitted.

The next day, Nani took Lilo to the animal shelter, hoping that a pet would help her little sister be less lonely. Lilo picked out a strange-looking dog and named him Stitch.

Stitch started causing problems right away. Nani wanted to take him back, but Lilo reminded her that Stitch was part of the family now.

"Dad said '*ohana* means family," she said. "Family means nobody—"

"Nobody gets left behind," Nani joined in. "Or forgotten."

Later Lilo, Stitch, and Nani went surfing with Nani's friend David. It was exactly like the kind of fun a real family would have. It made Lilo feel a little better.

That night, Lilo showed Stitch a picture of herself and Nani with their parents. Thinking about her parents always made Lilo sad. But having Stitch around made it a little easier. He was lonely, too. He needed Lilo the same way Lilo needed him. So, along with Stitch, Lilo also had her older sister and David. Together they made a family. And most important, she knew she would never be left behind or forgotten.

The Wedding Gift

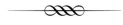

from *Aladdin and the King of Thieves*

Love is patient; love is kind.

Jasmine could not believe what had just happened. It was her wedding day. And just as the ceremony had gotten under way, the Forty Thieves had barged in on them! Together, Aladdin, the palace guards, and Genie had fought them off and driven them away—but the wedding had been ruined.

"What were they after?" Jasmine asked, still in shock. "The gifts?"

"Not *all* the gifts," Aladdin replied. He held up a short staff with a green gem at one end. During the struggle, he had seen the leader of the Forty Thieves trying to steal the staff. Aladdin was able to wrest it away. "*This* is what the King of Thieves wanted," he said.

Aladdin asked Genie about the staff.

"Oooh, looks like an oracle," Genie said.

Just then, the staff began to glow with a brilliant white light, and magically, a hazy female figure appeared, floating in midair. "I see all that has been and all that will be," the figure said. However, the Oracle explained, it could only answer one question for each person.

Jasmine realized the possibilities. "Aladdin, we could learn anything . . . about our lives, our future," she said.

"You have but to ask," the Oracle said.

Aladdin was more interested in knowing about his past than his future. "My mother died when I was just a kid," he said. "And I never even knew my father. I have no idea where I come from." But as Aladdin thought more about it, he realized that he had a million questions about his past; it would be impossible to choose just one. "I don't think you can help me," he said to the Oracle.

"Ah, but mere questions about your past can be answered by your father," the Oracle replied.

Aladdin was stunned. "My father? My father is alive?"

Aladdin needed some time to think. All his life, he had believed he was an orphan. This news changed everything. And yet, Aladdin was not sure he wanted to find his father. That evening, he and Jasmine talked it over.

"What kind of man leaves his son?" he said to Jasmine. "Did he even care? Maybe I don't want to know."

"Yes, you do," Jasmine replied.

"How can you be so sure?" Aladdin asked.

Jasmine smiled. "Because I already know him," she said. "Because I know you." Jasmine encouraged Aladdin to take advantage of this opportunity—to learn the truth, and the answers to all the questions he had about his father. And maybe, just maybe, to find his father and bring him to Agrabah in time for their wedding.

Finally, Aladdin was convinced. Together, he and Jasmine went to the Oracle.

"Where is my father?" Aladdin asked.

The Oracle immediately supplied the answer: "Follow the trail of the Forty Thieves. Your father is trapped within their world."

Aladdin was shocked and filled with worry. "The Forty Thieves?" he exclaimed. "Has he been hurt? How long has he been their prisoner?"

But the Oracle was bound by the rule of one. "I'm sorry. I can only answer one question," the Oracle replied.

Aladdin turned to Jasmine. "It's up to me," he said. Now that he knew of his father's predicament, Aladdin was doubly eager to find him.

Jasmine understood perfectly and supported Aladdin's decision. She wanted to marry Aladdin as soon as possible, but more than anything, she wanted what was best for him. She knew that the wedding could wait; this could not. Aladdin needed to make peace with his past.

"Take as long as you need," Jasmine said.

Silly, Romantic Ideas

from *Cinderella*

Follow your heart, no matter what others think.

The King was growing impatient with his son, the Prince. "It's high time my son got married and settled down," he complained to the Grand Duke. "I'm not getting any younger, you know."

"Now, now," the Grand Duke replied. "Perhaps if we just let him alone—"

"Let him alone?" the King shouted. "Him and his silly, romantic ideas?"

"But, sire, in matters of love—" the Grand Duke began.

"Love? Ha!" the King scoffed. "What is love? Just a boy meeting a girl under the right conditions. We must simply arrange the conditions."

The King decided to hold a ball and invite every eligible maiden in the kingdom. He sent messengers to deliver the invitations. A girl named Cinderella received one along with many other maidens throughout the kingdom.

Meanwhile, the Prince returned home and heard of the plans. Didn't his father understand? It wasn't meeting young ladies that was the problem, it was meeting a young lady that was special—one that made his heart flutter.

Still, he agreed to attend the ball. As one young lady after another came in and curtsied, the Prince grew bored. Would this evening never end?

He forgot such thoughts as he noticed another maiden enter the room. She was beautiful, but there was something more—something that made him push past the crowd of adoring maidens to get closer to her.

As he reached the beautiful maiden, he felt his heart flutter. Yes, he had been right. This one was special.

They danced without saying a word. The Prince and the beautiful maiden gazed at each other, not needing to speak. So this was what everyone always talked about, the Prince thought. So this was love. . . .

As the clock started to chime, the young lady suddenly gasped and pulled away. "Oh, my goodness!" she cried. "It's midnight! Good-bye . . ."

As she raced toward the front steps, the Prince followed. "Wait!" he cried desperately. "Please, come back! I don't even know your name—how will I find you?"

But the maiden didn't stop. A moment later she was gone, leaving behind only a single glass slipper that she had lost in her haste.

The Prince was heartbroken. Just when he finally understood true love, it had been ripped away. His father was still eager to see him married, so he ordered the Grand Duke to try the glass slipper on every maiden in the kingdom. The Prince would marry the first one it fit.

The Grand Duke tried the slipper on lady after lady, to no avail. Finally, he found his way to Cinderella's house. First he tried the glass slipper on her stepsisters, but it didn't fit them. Just as he was about to leave, Cinderella appeared. She tried the slipper on, and it fit perfectly. Cinderella was the Prince's true love.

The King wasted no time in arranging his son's wedding. He didn't want the Prince's dream girl to slip away again!

He needn't have worried. Neither the Prince nor Cinderella had any intentions of losing each other ever again.

Kuzco Gets a Clue

from *The Emperor's New Groove*

A true friend is a true treasure.

Emperor Kuzco stomped off to complain to the restaurant's chef, leaving his peasant guide Pacha to enjoy his fried pill bug in peace. Pacha was happily slurping away when he overheard whispering coming from the next booth.

"I should have done away with Kuzco when I had the chance!" hissed a female voice.

Pacha froze. Then he glimpsed Yzma, Emperor Kuzco's adviser. She was sitting with her assistant, Kronk, complaining about their botched plans. Now Pacha knew who was behind Kuzco's predicament!

Days earlier, Pacha had found Kuzco in the jungle. The Emperor was lost, alone, and stuck in the body of a llama. Still, even as a bewildered four-legged animal, Kuzco held on to his superior attitude. Pacha knew Kuzco would die if he left him to fend for himself, so Pacha agreed to guide the Emperor back to the palace. As their journey progressed—though neither would admit it—they had grown fond of each other.

Pacha knew he had to warn Kuzco right away, so he came up with a diversion to help Kuzco escape. He told the waitress it was Yzma's birthday. In the festive chaos that followed, Pacha dashed to the back of the restaurant to find his friend. But once Kuzco saw Yzma and Kronk, he wouldn't listen to Pacha any longer.

"I'm saved!" cried Kuzco happily.

"Trust me," Pacha said. "They're not here to save you. They're trying to kill you!"

But Kuzco had never had to trust anyone before. He had spent his entire life caring only about himself. And there was one thing he had never had before: a true friend. With all of his servants, subjects, and fancy things, he had never thought he needed one.

Kuzco dismissed Pacha and his warnings, and ran to catch up with Yzma and Kronk. But just before he reached them, he heard something that made him stop in his tracks.

"If you hadn't mixed up those potions," Yzma scolded Kronk, "Kuzco would be dead now!"

Kuzco dove behind a bush. Pacha was right! At that moment, he realized how foolish he had been—and how important it was to have a trusted friend. He turned

around to find the peasant, but he was gone. Forlornly, Kuzco went off into the jungle by himself.

Luckily for Kuzco, Pacha went out looking for him. Despite all of Kuzco's bad behavior, Pacha still wouldn't abandon him. Kuzco was overjoyed when he saw his one

and only friend. Together, they would find a way to turn Kuzco back into a human. But after what Kuzco had learned about friendship, he knew he would never turn back into his old self.

Twice Blessed

from *Sleeping Beauty*

---◦◦◦◦◦---

Love gives you the strength to do impossible things.

King Stefan and the Queen's joyous day had turned into their worst nightmare. The evil fairy Maleficent, angry at not having been invited to the celebration for the newborn Princess Aurora, had come, nonetheless, and had cast a dreadful spell upon the baby. True, the good fairy Merryweather had used her powers to soften the spell; but King Stefan still feared for his daughter's life. On her sixteenth birthday, Aurora was destined to prick her finger on the spindle of a spinning wheel and fall into a deep sleep, from which she could only be awakened by True Love's Kiss.

And so, seeking to protect his daughter, King Stefan ordered that every spinning wheel in the kingdom be burned. In the castle courtyard, they were piled high and lit with flaming torches.

The three good fairies, Flora, Fauna, and Merryweather, watched the bonfire from within the castle.

"Well," said Merryweather, "a bonfire won't stop Maleficent."

"Of course not. But what will?" Flora replied.

The fairies discussed ways they might use their magic to protect Aurora. But there were limits to their powers. As good fairies, they could not seek revenge on Maleficent. They could only use their magic to do good—to bring joy and happiness.

Flora had the idea to turn the princess into a flower, but decided that Maleficent would be expecting them to try something like that.

"Oh, well," said Merryweather. "What won't she expect? She knows everything."

Fauna disagreed. "Oh, but she doesn't, dear," she said. "Maleficent doesn't know anything about love or kindness or the joy of helping others."

"Of course!" Flora exclaimed. "It's the only thing she can't understand, and won't expect!" Flora went on to explain her plan: they would take Aurora away from the castle and raise her in secret, deep within the forest. Maleficent would never figure it out, especially if the fairies disguised themselves as mortals and lived without magic.

Merryweather was anxious about the plan. "We've never done anything without magic," she said.

"Oh, we'll all pitch in," Flora said.

At last, Merryweather agreed, because her love for Aurora was much greater than her uncertainty and fear.

"Come along now," said Flora. "We must tell Their Majesties at once."

Flora had predicted that King Stefan and the Queen would object to the plan—and she was quite right. But when the fairies explained that it was the only way to protect the princess, the royal parents knew what they had to do. With heavy hearts, they watched as the fairies took their only child and disappeared into the night. It was only their love for Aurora that allowed them to let her go.

And so, it just may be that on that night, baby Aurora was the most blessed child in all the land. For although she carried the burden of Maleficent's evil spell, she was so deeply loved by her parents and by the three fairies that they would undertake anything for her— including the impossible.

True-Blue

from *Monsters, Inc.*

⚋⚋⚋

Your friends are still your friends, even when you don't see eye to eye.

Sulley and Mike were best friends, roommates, and coworkers at Monsters, Inc. They bickered about a few things—like whether to walk to work or take the car. But they never argued about anything really important . . . until the day Sulley accidentally let a human child into Monstropolis.

Sulley and Mike managed to sneak the forbidden child into their apartment. Mike was nervous. "I bet she's just waiting for us to fall asleep and then *WHAM!* We're sitting targets!" he cried.

Sulley wasn't so sure. "This might sound crazy," he said, "but I don't think that kid's dangerous. Think about it. If we send her back, it's like it never happened. Everything goes back to normal."

"Sulley," Mike said, "that is a *horrible* idea!" He was sure there was no way to return the girl safely to her own world.

But Sulley wouldn't listen. The next day, he disguised the girl and brought her to the factory. Mike went with them, though he was very nervous.

"This is not okay, this is not okay, this is not okay!" he muttered. Still, he did his best to help as Sulley whisked the girl past the other monsters.

After running into a few mishaps, they went to Mr. Waternoose, the president of Monsters, Inc., for help. They tried to explain, but he grabbed the child and banished Mike and Sulley to a snowy wasteland in the human world.

"All you had to do was listen to me!" Mike shouted at Sulley. "Just once! But you didn't, did you?" He had never been angrier with his old friend.

Worse yet, Sulley *still* wasn't paying attention to him! All he cared about was getting back to Monstropolis to rescue the little girl.

"Nothing else matters," Sulley said. "I think there might be a way back."

"I don't want to hear about it," Mike replied. "You're on your own."

Sulley left without Mike. But Mike couldn't stay mad at Sulley for long. He followed him back to Monstropolis, just in time to save Sulley from his biggest rival, Randall.

"Look, you and I are a team," Mike said to Sulley. "Nothing's more important than our friendship."

Sulley was relieved. "I'm glad you came back, Mike," he said.

Working together, the two friends rescued the girl, and uncovered Mr. Waternoose's evil plot to kidnap children to collect their screams.

The girl was returned home, and the door to her room was shredded for safety reasons.

Sulley missed his little human friend. He spent a lot of time staring sadly at a picture she had drawn of him.

Mike had an idea. If he could figure out how to rebuild that door . . .

"Sulley," he said a few days later. "I want to show you something. . . . Ta-da!"

Sulley gasped when he saw the familiar door. "Mike? Is that her . . . ?"

Mike smiled. "Sorry it took so long, pal. There was a lot of wood to go through."

Sulley could hardly believe it. It was the best present he had ever received. And despite the occasional little argument—or even the occasional big fight—Mike was the best friend he had ever had.

Together Forever

from *Pocahontas*

---⊗⊗⊗---

Love transcends space and time.

Pocahontas *had* to get to the promontory before her father, Chief Powhatan, killed her beloved John Smith. Smith had taken the blame after another English settler shot an Indian warrior. Now Powhatan was going to avenge the killing by executing Smith.

Meanwhile, some English settlers led by Governor Ratcliffe were also moving toward the promontory. They, too, were intent on saving Smith. Both Pocahontas and the settlers arrived at the same moment, just as Chief Powhatan was raising his club over John Smith's head.

"No!" cried Pocahontas, throwing herself on top of Smith.

Powhatan halted his club in midswing and gazed down upon his daughter's face.

"If you kill him, you'll have to kill me, too," Pocahontas said.

"Daughter, stand back!" Powhatan ordered.

"I won't!" Pocahontas replied. "I love him, Father."

Powhatan's mouth dropped open in disbelief. He had no idea that Pocahontas had had several secret meetings with John Smith. The two were from very different worlds, but they had grown to know and love each other very much.

Pocahontas leaned closer to John Smith and pressed her head against his cheek. "This is the path I choose, Father," she said. "What will yours be?"

Powhatan looked around him and thought about Pocahontas's words. The chief did not want to set off a bloody battle. "From this day forward," he announced, "if there is to be more killing, it will not start with me." He ordered one of his warriors to release John Smith.

But Governor Ratcliffe was intent on a fight with the Indians. He grabbed a musket from one of the settlers and aimed it at Chief Powhatan.

"No!" cried John Smith. Smith lunged at Powhatan, knocking him out of the line of fire. The musket ball hit Smith instead!

"You shot him!" a young settler shouted at Ratcliffe. The settlers were shocked by Ratcliffe's behavior. They would no longer be led by such a brute. They surrounded Ratcliffe, carried him away, and put him in chains.

Meanwhile, Pocahontas tended to John Smith's wound. It was serious, and Smith's life was in danger. Soon, the settlers decided to take him back to London to receive medical treatment.

"Come with me?" John Smith asked as he lay in a stretcher.

Pocahontas looked at her father. "I'm needed here," she replied.

"Then . . . I'll stay with you," John Smith said.

Pocahontas knew that if he did, he would die. She loved him too much to let that happen. "You have to go back," she said.

"But I can't leave you," said John Smith.

Pocahontas smiled and gazed into his eyes. "You never will," she said. "No matter what happens, I'll always be with you. Forever."

Pongo Knows Best

from *101 Dalmatians*

Now and then, romance needs a nudge.

Pongo sat looking out the window while his "pet" Roger was hard at work at the piano, writing songs about romance—something Pongo thought Roger knew nothing about. If he did, they wouldn't be living alone together in Roger's messy bachelor flat. The two of them would be bachelors forever if it were left to Roger, thought Pongo. So the Dalmatian decided to take matters into his own paws. He was staring out the window, on the lookout for the perfect girl for Roger, when the most beautiful creature on four legs walked by. It was almost too good to be true: a gorgeous female

Dalmatian . . . and her lady was very lovely, too. Pongo watched as they headed for the park across the street from Roger's flat.

Pongo jumped off the window seat, got his leash, went to the door, and barked, begging Roger to take him for a walk.

"All right, boy," Roger said with a groan. As Roger put on his coat, Pongo fetched his hat and brought it to him. They had to get to the park as quickly as possible!

As soon as they were out the front door, Pongo strained hard at the leash, leading Roger straight into the park, up this path, and down that one, looking for the pretty lady with the beautiful Dalmatian.

"Pongo, old boy, take it easy," Roger said, puzzled at Pongo's behavior. "What's all the hurry?"

Finally, Pongo spotted them—the woman sitting on a bench, reading a book, and her dog right beside her. Pongo led Roger their way and strutted slowly past the bench. He thought he saw the two ladies looking up as they walked by. So far, so good, thought Pongo. Then he got the idea to grab Roger's hat and play "keep away" with it, just to attract the ladies' attention, and

for a while it seemed to work . . . until Pongo glanced over at the bench, and they were gone! And Roger began pulling Pongo in the direction of home!

But Pongo was not giving up. He took off, running after the ladies, with Roger clinging to the leash, being dragged along behind him. When he caught up to them, Pongo ran circles around the lady, twisting his leash around her legs and Roger's, until the two surprised humans were tied together.

"I beg your pardon," Roger said, tipping his hat to the lady.

"What on earth?" the lady replied. She grabbed Roger to try to keep herself from falling, but it was no use. They were off-balance, standing at the edge of a pond. An instant later, they both toppled with a splash into the shallow water.

Roger rushed to help the lady up, apologizing again and again. "He's never acted that way before," he said, gesturing at Pongo.

"Please, just go away," the lady replied impatiently. "You've done enough." She pulled a handkerchief out of her purse, only to find it soaking wet and no help at all.

"Oh, I say, here—take mine," Roger said as he took his equally wet handkerchief from his pocket and offered it to her.

A second later, they both started to laugh.

As they laughed, the beautiful Dalmatian smiled at Pongo for the first time and Pongo smiled back. He knew he and Roger wouldn't be bachelors for much longer.

O'Malley to the Rescue

from *The Aristocats*

———— ⊱⊰ ————

A good new friend feels like a good old friend from day one.

"Oh, I'll be so glad when we get back home," said Duchess as her new friend, Thomas O'Malley, led the way toward Paris. Duchess and her kittens, Marie, Berlioz, and Toulouse, lived in a grand mansion in the city. They were lost out in the countryside, but luckily, they had met O'Malley, and the tough alley cat had taken them under his wing.

As the cats walked along some train tracks, the kittens ran ahead of Duchess and O'Malley.

"Gee, whiz," exclaimed Berlioz, "look at that bridge!" They had come to a railroad bridge spanning a fast-moving river.

"Come on," said Toulouse, venturing far out onto the bridge. "Let's play train." He led the others along the tracks, making train noises as he went: "*Clickety, clickety, clickety . . . whoo, whoo!*"

Just then, a real train whistle sounded nearby. Halfway across the bridge, the kittens, Duchess, and O'Malley looked up to see a train barreling toward them from the opposite direction.

"Oh, no!" said Duchess with a gasp. There was no time to retrace their steps and get off the bridge!

"All right, now, don't panic," O'Malley said calmly. "Down underneath here." He jumped off the tracks and landed safely on a support plank that ran just underneath. Duchess and the kittens followed him, just in time. The train rushed overhead moments afterward.

Duchess was still catching her breath when she heard a call for help from far below.

"Mama!" It was Marie! In her rush to dodge the train, Marie had missed the support plank and fallen down into the river below. The tiny kitten struggled to stay afloat in the swift current.

"Keep your head up, Marie!" O'Malley shouted. "Here I come!"

Without a moment's hesitation, O'Malley dove off the bridge and into the water. He quickly paddled over to Marie, picked her up with his teeth, then dragged her over toward a floating log and grabbed hold of it.

Meanwhile, Duchess and the other kittens hurried off the railroad bridge and ran along the riverbank, keeping up with O'Malley and Marie as they were carried downstream. Then, outrunning the current, Duchess crawled out onto a limb hanging over the river.

"Thomas!" cried Duchess. "Thomas, up here!" As O'Malley and Marie floated by, clinging to the log, O'Malley flipped the kitten up to Duchess, who caught her in her mouth. At last, Marie was safe.

But poor O'Malley was still struggling in the water. Now that Marie was out of danger, O'Malley could concentrate on himself—and he realized that he didn't know how to swim!

"Thomas. Oh, Thomas, take care!" Duchess called out from the shore.

O'Malley was swept quickly along, still holding on to the log to stay afloat. Luckily, he met up with two geese downstream who fished him out of the water and helped him to shore.

"Oh, Thomas," said Duchess with relief. "Thank goodness you're safe." Although he had only known Duchess and the kittens for one day, O'Malley had risked his own life to save Marie. Duchess was beginning to think that this tough alley cat had one very soft heart.

A Prized Kiss

from *Robin Hood*

No matter how large the divide may seem, love can bridge the gap.

eep in Sherwood Forest, Robin Hood and Little John were tending to their chores, but Robin's mind kept wandering. He was shaken out of his daydream when the kettle boiled over.

"You're burning the chow," said Little John.

"Sorry, Johnny," Robin Hood replied. "I guess I was thinking about Maid Marian again. I can't help it. I love her, Johnny."

Growing up, Robin Hood and Maid Marian had been sweethearts. But now they lived very different lives. Maid Marian lived at the castle with her uncle, greedy Prince John. Robin Hood and his band of Merry Men lived as outlaws in Sherwood Forest, robbing from Prince John to feed the poor of Nottingham.

"Look," said Little John. "Why don't you stop moonin' and mopin' around? Just . . . just marry the girl."

"Marry her?" Robin Hood replied. "You don't just walk up to a girl, hand her a bouquet, and say, 'Hey, remember me? We were kids together. Will you marry me?' No.

It just isn't done that way." As much as Robin Hood loved Maid Marian, he was not sure they had a future together.

Still, when Robin Hood heard that Prince John was hosting an archery tournament, and that the winner would get a kiss from Maid Marian, Robin Hood entered right away. He and Little John dressed in disguise so that Prince John would not recognize them. Then, at the tournament, Robin Hood walked up to the royal box and handed a flower to Maid Marian.

"Ah, your ladyship," he said, disguising his voice as well. "Beggin' your pardon, but it's a great honor to be shootin' for the favor of a lovely lady like yourself." He winked at her. "I 'opes I win the kiss."

Maid Marian was certain that the spindly-legged stork was actually her beloved Robin Hood in disguise. She watched with delight as he handily won the archery tournament. Then Robin Hood stood before the royal box to collect his prize. He did not know that Prince John had discovered his true identity and was setting a trap to catch him.

"Archer," said Prince John, "I commend you, and because of your superior skill, you shall get what is coming to you." With a slash of his sword, Prince John cut off Robin Hood's disguise. "Seize him!" he shouted.

The guards tied up Robin Hood while Maid Marian pleaded with Prince John. "Please, have mercy," she begged.

"My dear emotional lady," the Prince replied, "why should I?"

"Because I love him, Your Highness," Maid Marian explained.

Prince John would not listen, but the words were music to Robin's ears—his Maid Marian loved him back!

With Little John's help, Robin Hood managed to escape. Then, with the guards hot on his heels, Robin Hood swung in on a vine and swept Maid Marian off her feet. They swung together onto the top of the royal box.

"Marian, my love," Robin Hood said, "will you marry me?"

Marian smiled. "Oh, darling, I thought you'd never ask me."

Then they escaped to Sherwood Forest, where Robin Hood gave Maid Marian an engagement ring made of flowers. At that moment, their lives did not seem so very different, after all.

The Ultimate Treasure

from *Aladdin and the King of Thieves*

⎯⎯∞⎯⎯

Family is worth its weight in gold.

Aladdin's father, Cassim, was in danger again. Cassim had been taken prisoner by Sa'Luk, one of the Forty Thieves. Sa'Luk was forcing Cassim to use the Oracle to find the ultimate treasure, the Hand of Midas—which turned everything it touched into gold.

Cassim, himself, had been after the treasure, and his greed had nearly destroyed his relationship with Aladdin. So, when Aladdin showed up, pounced on Sa'Luk, and freed him, Cassim was shocked.

"You came to help *me?*" he cried in disbelief.

"How could I do anything else?" Aladdin replied. Although Cassim had made mistakes, he was still family. "Now, let's get that treasure of yours!" Aladdin said.

Together, he and Cassim found the Midas Temple. Inside, on a golden platform suspended magically in midair, stood a stone statue of the legendary Midas. Cassim could see that one of the statue's hands was solid gold: the Hand of Midas.

Just then, a rush of water poured through a fountain in the temple wall. Time was running out!

Quickly, Aladdin and Cassim scrambled up the wall of the temple chamber. Then, Aladdin jumped onto the golden platform and without actually touching the treasure, he tossed the Hand of Midas to his father.

Cassim tested the treasure's powers by touching it to the water fountain on which he stood. Sure enough, the fountain turned to gold,

as did the waves of water pouring into the temple chamber. After years of searching, Cassim finally possessed the Hand of Midas!

But his good fortune did not last long. Sa'Luk had recovered and climbed up onto the golden platform. He stood menacingly over Aladdin as he shouted a threat at Cassim: "Give the Hand of Midas to me, Cassim, or your son dies!"

Aladdin advised his father not to give in. "Don't worry, Dad, I can take him alone!" he said confidently.

But Cassim had a plan. "You want the Hand of Midas, Sa'Luk?" he asked. "Take it!" With that, he threw the treasure across the chamber to Sa'Luk, who caught it in his bare hands. Then Sa'luk realized his fatal mistake. In seconds, his entire body had turned to solid gold.

Cassim and Aladdin recovered the treasure and climbed out of the flooding temple chamber. As they waited together on the temple roof for the Magic Carpet to pick them up, Aladdin congratulated his father. "After all these years," he said, "you finally have your treasure."

Cassim looked down at the Hand of Midas. "This thing?" he said. "No, this wretched thing almost cost me the ultimate treasure. It's you, son," Cassim said, smiling at Aladdin. "You are my ultimate treasure! I'm just sorry it took me this long to realize it."

Now that Cassim possessed the ultimate in riches, it became clear that these were not the things that made him feel the most blessed. Instead, it was family that did.

"The Hand of Midas can take its curse to the bottom of the sea!" Cassim exclaimed. And with a decisive fling of his arm, he threw the golden treasure into the vast sea.

The Wrong Buzz

from *Toy Story 2*

There's nothing like the real thing.

Buzz and the other toys were on a rescue mission. Woody had been stolen, and they suspected he might be at Al's Toy Barn. They reached the store and went inside. Looking around, they saw shelves stacked with thousands of toys.

"How will we ever find Woody in here?" Rex wondered.

Buzz told the others to look around. Meanwhile, he spotted a glowing green light nearby.

He followed it and found a display of brand-new Buzz Lightyear action figures. The New Buzz had a fancy utility pack with a grappling hook and other interesting gadgets.

Suddenly, the New Buzz reached out and grabbed Buzz. "Hi-yaaah!" he cried. The New Buzz said Buzz was in violation of space ranger code.

The two Buzzes fought. Buzz knew he didn't have time for this. He had to help save Woody!

But the New Buzz was stronger than he was. His improvements made him a better fighter. He wrestled Buzz to the

ground. Then he shoved him into his box and tied him down!

Buzz tried to escape, but the twist ties held him tightly. He watched helplessly as the New Buzz joined his friends. They didn't even seem to notice the difference!

"You've got the wrong Buzz!" Buzz shouted.

He banged on the box. But nobody heard him. Buzz finally broke free from the New Buzz's box, and he saw the toys leaving. He rushed out of the store after his friends.

Meanwhile, the other toys had no idea that the space ranger who was leading them wasn't their old friend Buzz. New Buzz was a good leader.

They reached Al's apartment building. "Troops!" New Buzz called, spotting a vent. "Over here!" He had seen that the vent traveled all the way up the building. They could reach Al's apartment that way.

Buzz caught up with them in Al's apartment. He saw the New Buzz carrying Woody over to the vent. Buzz knew he had to do something, so he flipped open the New Buzz's space helmet. The New Buzz dropped to his knees and gasped for air.

"I'm Buzz Lightyear!" said Buzz as he lifted his foot to show the word ANDY written on the bottom of his boot. The other toys then realized that he *was* the "real" Buzz.

"Let's go!" Buzz cried, rushing up to Woody.

"I can't, Buzz," Woody replied. "I'm part of a rare collectible set."

"You are a TOY!" Buzz shouted. He reminded Woody how much Andy needed him.

For a moment, Buzz didn't think Woody was going to listen. He had failed.

Then, a little boy appeared on the TV in the apartment. He reminded Woody of Andy. Buzz's words finally sank in. Woody realized that Andy *did* need him.

"Buzz, wait!" Woody cried. His old friend had done what no new-and-improved space ranger could do, no matter how many grappling hooks he had. Buzz had helped Woody remember what was really important.

THE POWER OF YOU

STORIES ABOUT HELPING OTHERS AND BEING YOURSELF

A Change of Heart

from *Dinosaur*

One selfless act can inspire another.

ladar and his friends were on their way to the Nesting Grounds when suddenly they stopped short and looked around in alarm.

"What was that?" Eema asked, as they cautiously crept forward to investigate the strange sound coming from up ahead.

Around the corner, they found Bruton, slumped against some rocks. He had deep battle wounds in his side and he was breathing heavily.

"Goodness gracious," Baylene said nervously after she recognized the dinosaur herd's second-in-command.

Bruton was not a welcome sight to Baylene and the others. Bruton, like many of the other dinosaurs, had never shown compassion for the weaker herd members. "Keep up!" he would always bark.

Baylene and Eema, being rather old, were often among those who weren't able to keep up with the rest of the herd.

"It appears we weren't the only ones left behind this time," Baylene observed.

Because Bruton had never shown concern for Baylene and Eema, they had little sympathy for him. But Aladar couldn't just leave Bruton to die.

"Let me help you," Aladar offered gently.

"Save your pity," Bruton said with a snarl. "Get away from me."

Just then lightning flashed. Aladar saw Url, Baylene's pet, go into a cave.

"If you change your mind, we'll be in those caves," replied Aladar.

It wasn't long before Bruton decided to seek shelter, too. He appeared at the entrance to the cave, grunting and panting. Then he collapsed.

"Come, come, on your feet," Aladar said as he pushed Bruton farther into the cave.

Baylene didn't understand Aladar's generosity toward Bruton. "May I remind you that he's one of *them?*" she said.

"Well, it looks like he's one of *us* now," Aladar replied.

Plio, one of Aladar's lemur friends, went over to tend Bruton's wounds. Bruton had never experienced such kindness before. These dinosaurs and lemurs had nothing to gain from helping him. Despite himself, Bruton's cold heart was beginning to warm toward these generous new friends.

The group was resting quietly, when, suddenly, two carnotaurs approached the cave. Aladar and the others slowly inched away from the cave entrance. It looked like the carnotaurs would pass them by, but then Baylene accidentally dislodged a rock from the cave wall. It rolled out of the cave and right into the predators' path. At once, the carnotaurs were upon them.

"Go! Go! Hurry!" cried Aladar, as everyone rushed to the back of the cave.

Soon the carnotaurs had Aladar pinned to the ground. Bruton ran and knocked them off Aladar. "I'll hold them off!" Bruton yelled to Aladar. "Help the others!"

Bruton knew that he didn't have the strength to beat two carnotaurs. Then he looked up and noticed that the archway above them was supported by one small column of rocks. He took a deep breath, and smashed right into the column. Heavy boulders came crashing down on the carnotaurs—and on Bruton.

"Bruton! No!" cried Aladar.

But it was too late. His new friend had put himself into mortal danger to save them. It was the ultimate act of friendship.

Under the Sun and Sea

from *The Little Mermaid II*

Sometimes love means making sacrifices.

Ariel had never regretted giving up her life as a mermaid to be with her beloved Prince Eric. Sometimes she missed the sea, but it was always there just outside the castle. All she had to do was step outside and splash in the waves or visit with her father and old friends who came up to the beach.

One day her life with Eric became even more joyful—they had a baby! Ariel named the child Melody, after the song that filled her heart whenever she looked into her baby's face. She couldn't wait to share the whole world with her daughter—on the land and under the sea.

The proud parents planned a grand celebration to introduce the baby to their family and friends. Eric's ship set off, while Ariel's father, King Triton, gathered the merpeople to welcome the new princess. Sebastian, Flounder, and other friends swam beside the ship, all of them eager for a glimpse of the brand-new baby.

King Triton had brought Melody a gift. "My precious Melody," he said, "I'm giving you this locket so you will never forget that part of your heart will always belong to the sea."

Triton was about to place the gift in his granddaughter's hand. But suddenly, an ugly black tentacle slithered out of the water and grabbed little Melody away from Ariel!

"Melody!" Ariel cried.

Morgana, the hideous sea witch, emerged from the waves, clutching the baby.

"Ursula's crazy sister!" Sebastian cried in horror.

Morgana had returned for revenge—Ariel and Eric had defeated her sister Ursula and foiled her plans to take over the undersea world. Now Morgana was going to pay them back by taking their daughter.

Eric and Triton acted quickly and snatched Melody back from Morgana's grasp.

"This isn't the end, Triton!" Morgana cried furiously. Then she disappeared beneath the waves.

Sadly, Ariel and Eric realized that Morgana would never rest until she got her slimy tentacles on Melody once again. There was only one solution—they had to keep Melody away from the sea.

They immediately built a tall, strong wall between the castle and the waves. Melody grew up safe and dry in the castle, never knowing the part that the sea had played in her life from the time before she was born.

Ariel still didn't regret giving up her life as a mermaid. But she did miss looking out at the waves and visiting with her father and old friends. But she knew she had no choice. As long as Morgana was out there, the sea meant danger for Melody. And Ariel was willing to make any sacrifice to keep her daughter safe.

Go for It!

from *A Bug's Life*

———❦———

When you believe in yourself, the sky's the limit.

Flik had been called before Princess Atta and her advisers.
"Flik, what do you have to say for yourself?" the Princess
demanded.

Flik had accidentally knocked over the huge pile of food that the
ants were forced to harvest for Hopper and his mean gang of
grasshoppers. Now the grasshoppers were demanding twice their
usual amount of food—by the end of the summer!

Flik hung his head. "Sorry," he mumbled. "I didn't mean for things to go so wrong." Flik always meant well and tried to do his best. But sometimes things didn't go exactly the way he had planned.

While Atta and the others discussed Flik's punishment, Flik had an idea. It was perfect! It would get those nasty grasshoppers off their backs forever!

"We could send someone to get help!" Flik exclaimed suddenly.

Atta was shocked by the idea. "Leave the island?" No ant in the colony had ever left Ant Island before.

"There's snakes and birds and bigger bugs out there," Thorny, one of Atta's advisers, pointed out.

"Exactly!" Flik replied. "Bigger bugs. We could find bigger bugs to come here and fight . . . and forever rid us of Hopper and his gang."

All the ants thought Flik was crazy. Besides, which ant would be silly enough to leave the island?

It wasn't until Flik volunteered to go that Princess Atta and her advisers changed their tune.

Dr. Flora whispered to Atta, "You see, with Flik gone . . ."

". . . he can't mess anything up!" Atta whispered back. The decision was made.

Flik was thankful for a chance to help the colony and make up for his blunder. As he set off from the anthill, many of the ants gathered to watch him go. "Don't worry!" Flik announced confidently. "The colony is in good hands!" Then he turned and strode on toward the edge of the island.

Two young ants caught up with Flik.

"My dad says he gives you one hour before you come back to the island, crying," one of them said to Flik.

The other one said his father predicted a far worse fate. "Yeah," he explained. "He says if the heat doesn't get you, the birds will."

Flik paid no attention to them. As they approached the edge of the dry ravine that surrounded Ant Island, little Princess Dot caught up with Flik.

"Well, I think he's gonna make it," Dot pronounced. She liked Flik. She had faith that he'd bring back the meanest, toughest bugs to battle Hopper. "He knows what he's doing."

"That's right!" Flik said as he shinnied up a dandelion stalk. At the top, he tore one wispy seed sack from the flower. "Here we go!" Flik shouted—"for the colony, and for oppressed ants everywhere!"

With that, he jumped off the flower, still clinging to the dandelion seed. It caught on a breeze and carried Flik through the air and across the ravine. So what if Dot was the only ant who thought he'd make good? Flik believed in himself, and that's what kept him going as he set off into the big, wide world.

Kida's Destiny

from *Atlantis: The Lost Empire*

Accept help from others, but also accept that there are things only you can do.

When Kida was only a child, she witnessed her mother sacrificing herself to save Atlantis from a tidal wave. The queen floated away into a huge crystal and never came back.

Years later, Atlantis was in trouble again. Its energy source was weakening, and its civilization was slowly crumbling away. One day, strangers from the surface world arrived in Atlantis. Kida watched them, wondering if they might be able to help.

Kida's father, the king, was not so happy to see the explorers. "Your heart has softened, Kida," he told her. "A thousand years ago, you would have slain them on sight."

"A thousand years ago, the streets were lit and our people did not have to scavenge for food at the edge of a crumbling city," Kida replied. "If these outsiders can unlock the secrets of our past, perhaps we can save our future."

The king sighed. "What they have to teach us, we have already learned."

But Kida could not agree with him. Milo Thatch, one of the explorers, was eager to help. He translated the ancient carvings Kida showed him and told her that the key to saving the city was a giant crystal called the Heart of Atlantis.

"It's what's keeping all of Atlantis alive," he explained.

"Then, where is it now?" Kida was confused.

Before they could figure it out, the captain of Milo's expedition showed up. Captain Rourke had heard about the Heart of Atlantis—and he intended to steal it to make his fortune!

Dragging Kida and Milo along, Rourke found his way to a chamber where a huge mother crystal floated above a pool of water. As Kida stared at the crystal, a beam of light shot out of it and landed on her. Feeling herself slip into a trance, Kida realized that the time had come to sacrifice herself, just as her mother had done.

Kida walked into the beams. "All will be well, Milo Thatch," she said. She began to crystallize, joining the Heart of Atlantis.

Some time later, after Milo and the Atlanteans had defeated Rourke, Kida returned to her normal state. She felt herself floating down until she landed in Milo's arms. She had never expected to see him—or anyone else—ever again. But the Heart of Atlantis had not needed to keep her as it had her mother. By offering herself for them, Kida had saved her people. Now she could live her life without worry—with her new friend Milo Thatch.

King-in-Training

from *The Lion King*

Be confident in yourself, but don't take unnecessary risks.

ufasa had warned his son Simba not to venture outside the Pride Lands. But then Simba's dastardly uncle, Scar, tempted the young lion by telling him of the elephant graveyard that lay beyond a rise at the northern border. Adventurous Simba just had to see it! Together with his friend, Nala, Simba went to explore the area.

"It's really creepy," said Nala as they walked up to a huge elephant skull.

"Yeah," Simba replied. "Isn't it great?"

"We could get in big trouble," Nala pointed out.

Simba chuckled. "I know," he said.

Just then, Zazu the bird caught up with them. It was his job to look after the young lions. Simba and Nala had been trying to lose Zazu all morning.

"We're way beyond the boundary of the Pride Lands," he told Simba. "And right now, we are all in very real danger."

Simba just smiled at Zazu. "I laugh in the face of danger. Ha-ha-ha-ha!"

From the shadows of the elephant skull, they heard other voices. Simba, Nala, and Zazu watched nervously as three hyenas emerged from the skull and walked toward them.

"Well, well, well, Banzai," said Shenzi the hyena. "What have we got here?" Shenzi recognized Zazu as Mufasa's assistant.

Banzai circled Simba and said, "And that would make you . . . ?"

"The future king!" Simba declared proudly.

The hyenas were unimpressed. "Do you know what we do to kings who step out of their kingdom?" Shenzi threatened.

At first, Simba was confident that the hyenas could not harm him. After all, he was Mufasa's son! Then Zazu explained that they were on the hyenas' land—and at their mercy.

Simba, Nala, and Zazu made a break for it, darting away from the hyenas and into the elephant graveyard.

"Did we lose 'em?" Nala asked Simba, panting.

"I think so," Simba replied.

But Zazu was missing! The hyenas had caught him. Simba and Nala went back for Zazu. They lured the hyenas away from Zazu, but then the hyenas started to chase them. Before long, the hyenas had the young lions cornered. Nala hid behind Simba as the hyenas closed in.

Suddenly, Mufasa leaped out of the shadows. His mighty roar echoed through the graveyard as he fought the hyenas. They were no match for the king and they pleaded for his mercy. Mufasa warned them to stay away from his son before letting them go.

Simba could barely look his father in the eye after what had happened.

"Simba, I'm very disappointed in you," Mufasa said when they got home. "You deliberately disobeyed me. And what's worse, you put Nala in danger."

Simba felt terrible. He began to cry. "I was just trying to be brave like you," he said.

Mufasa looked down at his son. "I'm only brave when I have to be," he explained. "Simba, being brave doesn't mean you go looking for trouble."

Simba still had a few things to learn about being a great king. But with his father as a role model and his loving guidance, Simba would someday have the strength and maturity to follow in Mufasa's footsteps.

Lost and Found

from *Lilo & Stitch*

Home is a feeling, not just a place.

Stitch was the only one of his species. A scientist named Jumba had created him as a terrible weapon.

The Galactic Council wanted to send Stitch away. "He is the flawed product of a deranged mind," they said. "He has no place among us."

Hearing that he was going to be sent away, Stitch decided he should escape.

Lilo had a home, but sometimes she felt as if she didn't belong there. She felt as if she didn't belong anywhere.

When Lilo saw a shooting star, she kneeled and wished for a friend who would understand.

Meanwhile, Stitch had escaped from the Galactic Council. He stole a spaceship and crash-landed on Earth. Someone found him and thought he was a dog, so he wound up in an animal shelter. The next day, Lilo came and adopted him.

Lilo brought Stitch to her house and showed him around his new home. "This is my room," she said. "And this is your bed." She pointed to a cardboard box.

Stitch looked around. Could this really be his new home?

Stitch started looking around Lilo's room and found a book with a picture of a small duck standing all alone. The caption read I'M LOST.

"That's the ugly duckling," Lilo explained. "He's sad because he is all alone and nobody wants him. But on this page his family hears him crying, and they find him. Then the ugly duckling is happy because he knows where he belongs."

Stitch thought about that. The ugly duckling had found where he belonged. Could Stitch do the same thing?

For the next few days, he tried to fit in at Lilo's house. But he kept causing more and more problems. Maybe he didn't belong there, either.

"If you want to leave, you can," Lilo told him sadly. "I'll remember you, though. I remember everyone who leaves."

Stitch took the book, *The Ugly Duckling*, and climbed out the window. He walked into the forest. He found a quiet, moonlit glade.

He looked up at the stars, then down at the book. "Los . . . los . . . lost," he said. "I'M LOST!"

The next morning, some members of the Galactic Council found Stitch in the forest. They wanted to lock him up, far away from everyone. "Don't make me shoot you!" Jumba warned. "Now, come quietly."

Stitch shook his head. "Waiting." He'd finally figured out where he belonged—with Lilo. Even though he hadn't come from Earth, she had helped him feel at home there. Even though he sometimes caused trouble, she was sad when he tried to leave.

Now that he'd found his true home, he never wanted to leave again.

On the Outside

from *Pocahontas II: Journey to a New World*

People should respect you for who you are—accept nothing less.

Pocahontas had traveled all the way to England to speak with King James I about making peace between the Indians and the settlers in Jamestown. Unfortunately, the king's wicked adviser Ratcliffe was set on making war. He cunningly convinced the king to invite Pocahontas to the fancy Hunt Ball. If Pocahontas was truly "civilized," Ratcliffe told the king, then she should easily fit in at the dance.

"It's the elite of British society," Pocahontas's friend John Rolfe explained. "If you slip up just once, Ratcliffe can convince the king . . ."

"Then I must not slip up," Pocahontas said, interrupting him. Pocahontas was determined to do whatever it took to show the king that her people deserved his respect.

That afternoon, Pocahontas was transformed from an Indian princess into a proper British lady. She wore a corset and powdered her face.

Just before they left for the ball, Rolfe presented Pocahontas with a gift: an English-style necklace. Pocahontas took off her traditional Indian necklace. "It doesn't belong here anymore," she said, as Rolfe fastened the new jewelry around her neck. Then she swept her long hair into a bun.

The king and queen were very impressed when they saw Pocahontas. She looked and acted just like one of them. But Pocahontas could only pretend for so long. When the king's entertainment included tormenting a chained bear, she had to voice her objections. She could change her clothes, but she couldn't change what was in her heart.

The king was so angered by her outburst that he had Pocahontas locked up in a tower. Her old love, John Smith, heard that she was in trouble and, along with Rolfe, helped her escape. Now Pocahontas had to decide what to do next: return to Jamestown, where war would inevitably break out, or try again to meet with the king?

Pocahontas ran off into the woods to think. When she saw her

reflection in a pond, she was ashamed. She hardly recognized herself. She washed off her powder and took down her hair.

At once, her resolve was strengthened. She would go to the king. If he couldn't respect her for who she really was, then his respect wasn't worth much.

Smith and Rolfe waited for her at the edge of the woods. Smith didn't want her to go before the king and queen.

"They're not going to listen to you. Look at you," Smith said, noticing Pocahontas's flowing hair.

"How can they respect my culture if they haven't even seen it?" she replied.

Unlike Smith, Rolfe understood Pocahontas's need to be true to herself and her people. He placed her old Indian necklace back around her neck. "I think it's time you taught society a lesson," he said encouragingly.

Then Pocahontas set off to see the king. If he still wouldn't speak to her about the trouble in Jamestown, then at least she would know she had represented her people with honesty and dignity. Working toward true respect and tolerance was the only way for a lasting peace.

Putting Friends First

from The Black Cauldron

───⟨∞∞⟩───

Good things happen when you put other people's needs before your own.

"Gurgi!" exclaimed Taran, when he saw that his furry friend had come to the rescue. "What—what are you doing here?"

Gurgi had managed to sneak inside the evil Horned King's castle and find his way to the chamber where Taran and his friends Fflewddur Fflam and Eilonwy were being held prisoner.

"Good boy, Gurgi," said Taran as Gurgi untied them all. "Eilonwy, you and Fflewddur go with Gurgi. I must stop the Cauldron!" The magical Black Cauldron had fallen into the hands of the Horned

King. He was going to use its awesome powers to take over all of Prydain! The only way to stop it was for someone to jump into the Cauldron of his own free will . . . never to come out alive.

"Please, Taran," said Eilonwy, realizing what Taran planned to do. "No! You can't!"

Gurgi tried to stand in Taran's way as he moved toward the steaming Cauldron, but Taran thrust him aside.

"If I don't, we're all lost," Taran replied. "Out of my way!"

But faithful Gurgi continued to protest. He turned away from Taran and before Taran could stop him, little Gurgi stepped off the ledge and tumbled down into the Black Cauldron.

"No-o-o!" shouted Taran as he watched his friend fall to his doom. Gurgi had sacrificed himself in order to save his friends and all of Prydain.

At once, the Horned King's castle began to catch fire and crumble. The Horned King's hold over the Black Cauldron was broken; now the Cauldron wanted *him*. A swirling wind overpowered the Horned King, drawing him to the Cauldron, and pulling him inside, never to be seen again.

Taran, Fflewddur, and Eilonwy barely managed to escape from the castle before it collapsed into the lake. In an old boat, they rowed to safety on the far shore. Then, as the smoke and fog cleared, Taran looked out across the water and spotted the Black Cauldron floating

nearby. He fell to his knees in despair as he thought about what Gurgi had sacrificed.

"Why didn't I stop him?" Taran said to himself.

Just then, the three witches, Orgoch, Orddu, and Orwen, appeared to Taran. Before the Black Cauldron had fallen into the Horned King's hands, Taran had bargained with the witches to get the Cauldron. Now they wanted it back. In exchange, they offered Taran a magnificent sword. Taran rejected the trade.

"But I would trade it . . ." Taran began.

"Yes . . . yes?" said the witches, eager to hear his counteroffer.

"The Cauldron for Gurgi," said Taran hopefully.

The witches whirled around the Cauldron, lifting it out of the water. As it rose, it dissolved to a brilliant white light that gradually

turned into a spiraling, darkening sky. Taran, Fflewddur, and Eilonwy watched as the whirlwind touched down on the shore. The next thing they knew, the witches were gone . . . and Gurgi lay before them on the ground.

Taran ran to Gurgi's side, but Gurgi did not move. A tear welled up in Taran's eye and ran down his cheek. He put his arms around Gurgi and hugged him.

That's when Taran felt Gurgi's hand reach into his vest pocket.

"Gurgi! You're alive!" Taran exclaimed.

A wave of relief washed over Taran. Gurgi was safe and sound. The Horned King was defeated. And, after showing how much they cared for each other, Taran and Gurgi would surely be friends forever.

Romancing Roxanne

from *A Goofy Movie*

Being yourself is the coolest way to be.

It was the last day of school before summer break, and Max's last chance to impress Roxanne, the girl he liked. He was leaving nothing to chance.

For weeks, Max and his friends had been planning an enormous surprise. During assembly, they took over the auditorium and performed their own version of their favorite band's hit video. Max dressed up like the pop star from Powerline and danced and lip-synched. The show went off without a hitch. All of the kids loved it—including Roxanne.

Later that day, Max ran into her in the hall. He took a deep breath. "Um, Roxanne, I was sorta, kinda thinking that maybe I'd . . . um . . . ask you to go with me . . . that is, to the party. Of course, if you don't want to, I'd completely understand."

"I'd love to," said Roxanne.

Max couldn't believe it! It was a dream come true.

But the dream didn't last long. When he got home from school, his dad Goofy told him they were going on a surprise fishing trip—and they were leaving for Lake Destiny that very day. Max was going to miss the party.

He went over to Roxanne's house to tell her the bad news. Roxanne said it was okay, that she would just find someone else to go with.

"Someone else?" asked Max, crushed by the idea. "Um, Roxanne, my dad's taking me to the Powerline concert in L.A.!" Max couldn't stop himself. "So, you aren't still thinking of going with someone else, are ya? Because I was hoping to wave to you onstage when we join Powerline for the final number!"

"This is incredible!" Roxanne said.

"Well, I wouldn't miss our date for anything that wasn't incredible, Roxanne," Max said.

Max waved good-bye and walked down to where Goofy was waiting in the car. He didn't know how he was ever going to get himself out of this whopper.

Over the next couple of days, Max tried everything to reroute their road trip from Lake Destiny to L.A. He was miserable, and all of his plans backfired. Finally, he told Goofy the whole embarrassing story. Much to Max's surprise, his dad agreed to take him to L.A., and to help him get onstage with Powerline. To his even greater surprise, Goofy's plan actually worked! All of the kids at the party saw him dancing on TV.

But on their drive back home, Max decided he had to tell Roxanne the truth.

"You're doing the right thing, son," Goofy told him.

"Yeah, I know. But she'll probably never talk to me again," Max replied gloomily.

"Well, if she doesn't, maybe she's just not the one for you," Goofy said, as he dropped Max off at Roxanne's door.

When he saw Roxanne, Max immediately told her about the lie. "Why would you make up something like that?" she asked.

"I guess I just wanted you to like me," he answered sheepishly.

"But I already liked you, Max," Roxanne answered.

Max was even happier than he had been before. All this time he thought he needed to pretend to be cool to get Roxanne to like him. But she liked him for who he was—and being himself was easy.

Who's the Real Thief?

from *The Little Mermaid II*

⸺ ⧜ ⸺

Trust your first impressions.

Ariel's daughter, Melody, was thrilled when Morgana magically turned her into a mermaid. There was just one problem.

"There wasn't enough potion for this to be a *forever* spell," Morgana said sadly. "I could make the spell last longer if I had my magic trident. But it was stolen years ago, and there's no one to get it back for me."

Melody couldn't stand the thought of returning to her ordinary life. "Maybe I could get it back for you," she suggested.

"You would do that for me?" Morgana asked.

"I'll bring you back your trident," Melody promised.

With the help of her new friends Tip and Dash, Melody found her way to Atlantica. They sneaked into King Triton's castle and hid beneath a table.

Melody peeked out, just as King Triton had entered. "That must be him," Melody whispered to her friends. "He looks sad—he doesn't look like a thief."

Melody stared at the merman. Despite the fact that Morgana had told her that King Triton had stolen the trident, she couldn't shake the feeling that he was a good person. He looked so thoughtful and kind.

Suddenly, she spotted the trident. "Look, there it is!"

When Triton left the room, Melody swam over to the trident. It was beautiful—and oddly familiar. Why did she feel so strange when she looked at it?

"The king's coming back!" cried Dash.

Melody shook off the strange feeling and grabbed the trident. Then she and her friends swam to safety.

Morgana was waiting back in her cave. "There you are, darling," she cooed. "Look, you've brought my trident! Clever girl."

Melody handed over the trident. As soon as she touched it, Morgana began laughing maniacally.

"All the power of the seven seas is now at my command!" she cried. "And little Melody's been a very naughty girl—stealing from her own grandfather!"

Melody gasped. "My *grandfather?*"

She felt terrible. The nice-looking merman hadn't stolen the trident from Morgana. Instead, Morgana had convinced her to steal it from him. She should never have trusted Morgana or gone against her own instincts.

As Morgana turned Melody back into a human, Ariel and King Triton showed up, along with their friends. But the trident gave Morgana the power to command everyone of the sea.

Suddenly, Melody realized something—with her legs back, she was no longer of the sea! She might be the only one who could defeat Morgana. And this time she wasn't going to ignore her instincts. She sneaked up and grabbed the trident away from Morgana, returning it to King Triton.

Melody still felt bad about helping Morgana. But her family was quick to forgive her. She hugged her grandfather for the first time.

Now she would no longer have to choose between the land and the sea. With Morgana defeated and her family together again, she could have the best of both worlds!

Stay or Go?

from *Tarzan*®

Sometimes you have to be willing to give up everything you've ever known to get everything you've ever wanted.

In all his days in the jungle, Tarzan had never met anyone like Jane. She answered many of his questions, and taught him all about how to be a human. But one day, Tarzan learned that Jane was leaving. She was returning to her home in England, far across the ocean with her father, Clayton, and his crew of men.

"We really hope that you'll come with us," Jane told Tarzan. "Won't you?"

Tarzan was excited. Jane had shown him so many new and fascinating things already.

"Go see England today," he said eagerly. "Come home tomorrow?"

Jane looked worried. "Oh, no," she said. "You see, it would be very difficult to come back. Ever."

Tarzan couldn't imagine such a thing. Leave his home—forever? He had a better idea.

"Jane stay with Tarzan." He knelt and handed her a jungle flower. Jane dropped the flower, looking stunned. "Stay here?" she said.

"Jane. Stay." Tarzan said as he picked up the flower and handed it to her again. "Please."

Jane started to cry. "But—I can't. . . ." She ran off.

Tarzan tried to change Jane's mind by taking her to meet his gorilla family. He even taught her to speak gorilla.

"*Oo-oo-ee-eh-ou,*" he demonstrated.

"Oo-oo-ee-eh-ou," she repeated. "What did I say?"

"That Jane stays with Tarzan," Tarzan told her.

Still, Jane would not agree to stay. Finally, Tarzan made a difficult decision. He would leave his own world and live in hers.

"Tarzan!" Jane cried happily when she saw him coming toward the ship. As he came aboard, she chattered excitedly. "You can't imagine what's in store for you. You're going to see the world!"

"And I'll be with Jane," Tarzan said. To him, that was the most important thing.

Jane was touched by his words. "Yes," she said softly. "With Jane."

As Tarzan looked out over the jungle one last time, Clayton and his evil companions grabbed Jane, her father, and the rest of the crew. It was mutiny!

Tarzan tried to escape, but the men seized him. He overheard their plan to capture his ape family and put them in cages. Realizing he had helped make it possible by taking Jane and the others to meet the gorillas, Tarzan let out a wild cry of despair.

Luckily, his friends Tantor and Terk heard his cry. They helped Tarzan escape, and together they defeated the villains. But the apes' leader was killed in the fight. With his dying breath, he asked Tarzan to look after the family.

Once again, the ship prepared to leave. But this time Tarzan was not on it. He couldn't leave when his family needed him. Jane understood, but her heart ached as she said good-bye.

She boarded the ship. But she couldn't stop staring at Tarzan back on shore.

Her father took her hand, "Jane, dear, I can't help feeling that you should stay," he said.

"We've been through all that, Daddy," replied Jane. "I couldn't possibly let you go—"

"I'll be fine!" her father insisted. "And you're in love with him."

Jane realized her father was right. Still, she couldn't imagine giving up all she'd ever known to stay in the jungle.

"Sometimes risking everything is the most sensible thing to do," her father said gently.

Once again, Jane realized he was right. She had to follow her heart. Hugging her father one last time, she leaped overboard and waded to shore.

Tarzan was waiting for her with his ape family.

Jane smiled at the apes. "*Oo-oo-ee-eh-ou,*" she said.

The apes cheered. Jane's heart soared. Her decision had not been easy, but she knew she would never regret it.

Temper, Temper

from *Beauty and the Beast*

⊷⊶

A bad mood does nobody any good—least of all, you!

The Beast was almost always angry. He had once been a prince, but a sorceress had changed him into a hideous creature. He was only allowed to view the outside world through a special enchanted mirror. If he didn't break the spell soon, he would be trapped in his new form forever.

One day, a visitor came to the castle—a man named Maurice. The Beast was sure he had come to stare at him, so he locked him in the dungeon.

Maurice's daughter, Belle, came looking for her father. She offered to become a prisoner in his place. The Beast was surprised that anyone would do such a thing, but he agreed.

As he led Belle to her room, Lumiere, the candelabrum, nudged him. "Say something to her!" he urged.

The Beast cleared his throat. "The castle is your home now," he told Belle. "You can go anywhere you like—except the West Wing. It's forbidden!" the Beast roared. Then remembering that he was supposed to be polite, he invited Belle to dinner.

But when the dinner hour came, there was no sign of Belle. The Beast paced and growled as he waited.

"Try to be patient, sir," Mrs. Potts, the teapot, said.

The Beast wasn't patient—especially when he discovered that

Belle didn't plan to come to dinner. "Fine!" he shouted angrily. "If she doesn't eat with me, she doesn't eat at all!"

Later that night, the Beast found Belle in the forbidden West Wing. The Beast lost his temper completely.

"GET OUT!" he roared at the top of his lungs.

Belle gasped with fright. She raced out of the room—and straight out of the castle.

Realizing he'd made a mistake, the Beast went after her. He found her just in time to fight off a pack of wolves that had surrounded her.

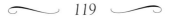

Back at the castle, Belle put a hot towel on his wound.

The Beast roared with pain. "That hurts!"

"If you'd hold still, it wouldn't hurt as much!" she snapped, losing her own temper.

"Well, if you hadn't run away, this wouldn't have happened!" the Beast responded.

Belle didn't back down. "If you hadn't frightened me, I wouldn't have run away."

"Well, you shouldn't have been in the West Wing," said the Beast.

"Well, you should learn to control your temper!" she said. The two glared at each other for a moment. Then Belle held up the towel again and gently cleaned the wound. "By the way—thank you for saving my life."

The Beast was surprised, but pleased. "You're welcome," he replied.

After that, a funny thing happened. The Beast found it easier to control his temper when Belle was around. Now he found himself smiling, and laughing, and having fun—things he hadn't done in a long, long while. And that was a much nicer feeling than being angry all the time.

OPEN YOUR MIND

STORIES ABOUT FAIRNESS AND GOOD JUDGMENT

Life Lessons

from *Tarzan*®

Always be open to learning new things—even in the most unusual places.

Young Tarzan knew he was different from the other animals in the jungle. But he was determined to fit in as best he could. He observed all the different species and tried to adopt their best qualities—the strength of an elephant, the fearlessness of a rhinoceros, the agility of a baboon. By the time he had grown up, Tarzan was as strong and fearless and agile as any of the other animals.

Then, one day, Tarzan had his first encounter with animals that looked like him—humans! They had come from far across the ocean. One of them, a pretty young woman named Jane, was eager to learn all she could about gorillas and their habitat.

Tarzan watched as Jane wandered through the jungle, observing the animals she saw. As Jane sketched in her sketchbook, a baby baboon grabbed the picture from her. Jane snatched it back and a group of angry baboons began to chase her. Luckily, Tarzan saved her.

Once they were safe, Tarzan decided to try to speak to her. He pointed to himself.

"Tar-zan," he said.

Jane pointed to herself and said, "Jane."

They stared at each other in wonder. Neither really understood the other—yet—but they both wanted to know more.

Back at the human camp, Jane introduced Tarzan to her father and their guide. Tarzan looked at the two men curiously, noticing how they stood upright. He imitated their stance. It felt . . . different. But good!

Tarzan realized he had only begun to learn all the things he needed to know. He eagerly listened and watched as Jane and her father taught him to speak in their language. He studied their drawings. He gazed through their telescope. Jane even taught him how to dance!

But Tarzan wasn't the only one who was learning. Jane could hardly believe how many things the ape-man had to teach her. Tarzan brought her high into the trees, showing her his world. He coaxed beautiful jungle birds to perch on her arms. He even taught her how to speak to the gorillas!

Jane wasn't sure whether she was learning more from Tarzan, or he from her. But it really didn't matter. The important thing was that they both had lessons to teach and to learn.

And both of them knew that the new knowledge they were gaining from each other could only make their lives better.

Friend or Foe

from *The Lion King II: Simba's Pride*

Judge each individual on his or her own merits.

Kiara was ready to go exploring one day when her father, Simba, stopped her. "Remember," he said, "I want you to stay in sight of Pride Rock—"

"—at all times," Kiara finished teasingly. "I know. And if I see any strangers, don't talk to them. Okay, okay, can I go now?"

Simba smiled. But he had one more warning. "Stay away from the Outlands."

His adviser, Zazu, nodded. "Nothing there but a bunch of murderous Outsiders," he said.

After agreeing to be careful, Kiara ran off. She wasn't sure why her father was so worried about Outsiders—he wouldn't tell her anything about them. The only thing he would say was that she should never turn her back on one.

She wandered through the Pride Lands, looking for something fun to do. Suddenly, she noticed that her father's friends Timon and Pumbaa were following her.

Kiara was annoyed. Her father must have sent the pair to watch her. She didn't need baby-sitters!

It wasn't hard to lose Timon and Pumbaa. But when she did, Kiara realized that she was lost. She was looking for a way home when she came upon another lion cub—one she didn't recognize. He had to be an Outsider!

Kiara snarled. "My father says never to turn your back on an Outsider," she said.

"You always do what Daddy says?" asked the stranger. "An Outsider doesn't need anybody. I take care of myself."

As they argued, a nearby log moved. Kiara gasped, realizing it wasn't a log—it was a hungry crocodile! And there wasn't just one—there were lots of crocodiles.

Kiara and the strange lion leaped away in terror. The crocodiles chased them, but they helped each other escape. When they were safe, the two cubs danced with excitement.

"You were really brave," Kiara said. "I'm Kiara."

"You were pretty brave, too," the other cub replied. "My name's Kovu."

From that moment on, the two cubs were no longer strangers to each other. It didn't matter that Kiara was a Pride Lander and Kovu was an Outsider. They were friends.

A Very Special Pig

from *The Black Cauldron*

Never judge a book by its cover.

In a tiny corner of the land of Prydain, just outside old Dallben's cottage, young Taran was tending to his chores. It was time for him to feed Dallben's pig, Hen Wen.

Taran made a disgusted face after giving Hen Wen her gruel. "Is that to be my life?" he said. "Eh? Pampering a pig?" Taran picked up a stick that was lying nearby and wielded it as if it were a mighty sword. "All I need is a—is a chance. And I could be a famous warrior!" he cried.

Taran pretended that Dallben's goat was the evil Horned King. He rattled his stick between the goat's horns, and was congratulating himself on his victory when the goat rammed him and knocked him into a mud puddle. Taran looked up to find Dallben standing over him.

"Another dream, Taran?" the old man asked.

"Dallben, won't I ever be anything but an assistant pig keeper?" asked Taran.

"She's a special pig, Taran," said Dallben. Then he asked Taran to give her a bath.

Taran picked up Hen Wen and put her in a barrel of water. She loved having her back washed. Hen Wen seemed content—until suddenly, she sat up with a start, then leaped out of the barrel and darted away. Taran chased after her. Inside the cottage, Dallben heard the commotion and looked out the window. "Taran, what's going on?" he called.

Taran finally caught the pig and held on to her tightly. She was shaking from head to toe. "There's something wrong with Hen Wen," Taran replied.

"Quickly, lad," Dallben instructed, "bring her inside."

Taran did as he was told.

"What's that for?" Taran asked, pointing to a pail of water Dallben had placed in the center of the room.

"I never use Hen Wen's powers unless I have to. But now I must," replied Dallben.

"Powers?" Taran said.

The old man began to stir the water in the pail with his long staff.

Hen Wen stepped forward and touched her snout to the spinning water. At that, the water began to glow and a vision took shape—a vision of the wicked Horned King searching desperately for the Black Cauldron.

"It's been hidden for centuries," Dallben told Taran. "But if the Horned King should find it and unleash its power, nothing could stand against him."

Then an image of Hen Wen appeared in the water. Dallben gasped. "He knows," Dallben said, his eyes wide. He pulled Hen Wen away from the pail, shaking her out of her trance. "You must leave here at once!" he said, and then instructed Taran to take Hen Wen and keep her

hidden in the forest. "Only I knew the secret of Hen Wen's power, but now the Horned King has discovered it," Dallben explained to Taran. "We must be sure he never uses it to find the Black Cauldron."

Minutes later, Taran and Hen Wen were setting off into the countryside.

"Gosh, Hen Wen," Taran said as they walked. "I never knew you could create visions and things like that. I thought you were just an ordinary pig."

Soon Taran would learn firsthand that, with an extraordinary pig in his charge, the life of a pig keeper was quite an adventure, indeed.

Home Is Where the Heart Is

from *The Aristocats*

Don't knock it till you've tried it.

It was time for Duchess and O'Malley to go their separate ways, but they could not find the right words.

"I don't know what to say," Duchess said. She and O'Malley were very different: Duchess was an aristocat who lived in a Paris mansion with her adoring owner, Madame Bonfamille, while O'Malley was an alley cat from the countryside. But in the short time since they

had met, the two cats had grown very fond of each other. O'Malley had helped Duchess and her three kittens find their way home after Madame's butler, Edgar, had abandoned them out in the country.

Now, at last, the cats had arrived home. The kittens ran to the door while Duchess and O'Malley said their good-byes.

"Maybe just a short, sweet good-bye would be easiest," O'Malley suggested.

Duchess wished that O'Malley would stay. But O'Malley had a thing about humans. He did not believe that they truly cared about their pets.

"Well, I guess they won't need me anymore," O'Malley said as he watched Duchess and the kittens walk into the house.

Little did O'Malley know how much the cats really needed him—at that very moment! Seconds after they walked through the front door, Edgar trapped them in a large sack. He was determined to get

rid of them for good. Once they were out of the way, Edgar would become the sole heir to Madame's estate.

Luckily, Roquefort the mouse saw that the cats were in danger and ran after O'Malley.

"Duchess . . . kittens . . . in trouble," Roquefort managed to say, all out of breath. "Butler did it."

O'Malley sprang into action. He sent Roquefort to get help from O'Malley's alley-cat friends while he raced to Madame's. He arrived in time to see Edgar carrying the sack of cats into the barn. There the butler locked them inside a steamer trunk. He was planning to ship Duchess and the kittens all the way to Timbuktu! "And this time,

you'll never come back!"
Edgar said with a nasty
chuckle.

But O'Malley had other
ideas. He got inside the
barn and climbed up into
the loft. Then he jumped
down onto Edgar and
knocked him over. Edgar
recovered, grabbed a
pitchfork, and chased after
O'Malley. But soon Roquefort arrived with Scat Cat and several other alley cats. They ganged up on Edgar while Roquefort freed Duchess and the kittens from the trunk.

Then, working together, the alley cats forced Edgar over to Frou Frou the horse, who kicked the butler across the barn and into the trunk. The lid slammed shut. Soon a truck arrived to pick up the trunk, and Edgar was on his way to Timbuktu!

When Madame discovered that Duchess and the kittens were back, she was so relieved that she asked O'Malley to stay. "We need a man around the house," she said.

After nearly losing Duchess and the kittens, O'Malley decided that he couldn't bear to leave them again. And once he met Madame, he realized he had been wrong about humans. Not only did Madame welcome O'Malley, she also took in all of his alley-cat friends. If that wasn't caring, O'Malley didn't know what was.

Oh, and living in a mansion wasn't all bad, either.

Puppies, Puppies, Everywhere!

from *101 Dalmatians*

---✇---

The more, the merrier!

At last, Pongo and Perdy, along with ninety-nine Dalmatian pups, were on their way home. They were still covered in the soot they had used to disguise themselves so they could sneak away from that nasty Cruella De Vil. Cruella had dognapped ninety-nine Dalmatian puppies, including Pongo and Perdy's pups, and plotted to use their spotted fur to make a coat! Luckily, Pongo and Perdy had arrived at Cruella's hideout in time to rescue them all, and although Cruella had chased after the escaping dogs, she had crashed her car during the pursuit. Finally safe, the dogs were stowed

away in the back of a moving van, headed back to Roger and Anita's house in London.

Meanwhile, Roger and Anita tried to make the best of their Christmas without their beloved dogs. But it was hard to be cheerful. "I still can't believe that Pongo and Perdy would run away," Roger said.

Their housekeeper, Nanny, was also upset about the dogs' absence. "Sometimes at night I can hear them barking. But it always turns out I'm dreaming," she said with a little sniff.

Just then, Nanny, Roger, and Anita *did* hear barking . . . coming from outside. Nanny ran to open the front door and was forced back into the room as Pongo and Perdy jumped up on her and then bounded into the house with the puppies in tow.

"Why, they're Labradors," said Roger.

But Nanny held up her apron, which had a black paw print on it. "No, they're covered in soot," she said.

Roger took a handkerchief and wiped off Pongo's face. "Oh, Pongo, boy, is that you?" he exclaimed with delight.

Anita wiped Perdy's face with her apron and hugged her. "And Perdy, oh, my darling!" she cried.

Nanny proceeded to dust off Pongo and Perdy's puppies. There was Patch, Rolly, Penny, Freckles, little Lucky, and all the others. "And look," said Nanny, scanning the room. "There's a whole lot more."

Anita could hardly believe her eyes. "There must be a hundred of them!" she said.

Together, Roger, Anita, and Nanny started counting. There were thirty-six pups on the stairs, eleven on the chair, eighteen on the window seat, six behind the couch, and thirteen more that were being dusted off by Nanny.

"Let's see now," said Roger, doing some quick math. "That's eighty-four." He added Pongo and Perdy and their fifteen pups, which brought the grand total to . . .

"One hundred and one!" said Anita. "Where'd they all come from?"

And what would Roger and Anita do with them all? Pongo and Perdy and their puppies had been quite a lot of dogs to begin with. Did they have room in their lives for one hundred and one Dalmatians?

Roger did not hesitate for a moment. "We'll keep 'em!" he declared. "We'll buy a big place in the country!"

The dogs barked their agreement. Roger and Anita hugged. Then Roger tiptoed his way through the puppy-filled room and sat down at the piano. He began to sing a song about their new life out in the country, in a home made all the more happy and loving by their new family members—all eighty-four of them!

Blessing From Above

from *Dinosaur*

Don't let fear close your heart to someone who needs you.

At last, the dinosaur egg's long journey had come to an end. It had been snatched up by a pterodactyl and flown across the sea to Lemur Island, where it had accidentally been dropped into some trees. The lemurs who made their home in the treetops scattered in all directions as the strange object dropped out of the sky. Then, when all was quiet again, they peeked through the leaves to see that it had landed atop a soft mound of moss on one of the branches.

"Yar," whispered Zini, one of the young lemurs, "what is it?"

"I don't know," wise old Yar replied.

Yar's daughter, Plio, was determined to find out. She inched out onto the tree branch. Then, reaching the mossy mound, she leaned in to examine the object. As she did, it began to wiggle—and crack open!

Plio leaned in some more and peered at the newly formed crack in the surface of the object.

"Dad," she called over her shoulder to Yar, "get over here."

Yar made his way slowly out onto the branch. "Well, what is it?" he asked.

With her back still to him, Plio replied, "It *was* an egg." Then she turned to face her father. She was cradling a tiny, newly hatched iguanodon in her arms.

Yar pulled back in shock at the sight of the creature. "It's a cold-blooded monster from across the sea—vicious, flesh-eating!" Yar exclaimed.

Plio shrugged. "Looks like a baby to me," she said.

"Babies grow up," Yar replied, raising his voice. "You keep that thing—one day we'll turn our backs . . . it'll be picking us out of its teeth!"

Plio looked down at the helpless little creature in her arms. "So, what do we do?" she asked Yar.

"Get rid of it!" Yar snapped.

Defensively, Plio shielded the baby from Yar's outburst. Then, as Yar turned away, Plio looked at him disapprovingly. "What has gotten into you?" she said.

"Plio," Yar replied, "that thing is *dangerous*."

Plio was quiet for a few moments. Then she handed the little creature to Yar, saying, "Okay, get rid of it." She knew Yar wouldn't have the heart to harm the creature.

Yar held the baby awkwardly. He carried him to the edge of the branch and held him out so the baby was dangling high above the forest floor. All Yar had to do was to let go and the dinosaur would be out of the lemurs' lives forever.

But Yar hesitated. Holding the baby out in front of him, Yar was face-to-face with the defenseless creature. The baby looked up into Yar's eyes, then yawned. He seemed right at home in Yar's arms. In those few moments, the little dinosaur worked his way into Yar's heart.

Yar turned and handed the dinosaur back to Plio. He watched as Plio carried the baby off to tend to him. "Watch his head!" Yar exclaimed protectively. Then, trying to hide his warm feelings, he said, "I mean . . . watch it. He could bite."

Plio cradled the baby while the other lemurs gathered around to meet the new addition to their clan. "Look at that sweet little face," Plio cooed. "Does that look like a monster to you?"

The Odd Couple

from *Monsters, Inc.*

Being different doesn't have to mean being scary.

ll over the world, bedtime follows the same pattern.

"Good night," a child says.

"Good night!" the parents reply.

The lights are turned off. Suddenly, the familiar bedroom is filled with scary shapes and shadows. Is that something moving over there? What is that sound under the bed? Can the closet door really be creaking open?

"*Aaaaaaaah!*" the child screams as a monster leaps out and roars. The monster is so strange, so terrifying, that the only response is

to scream and hide. If the child only knew that the monster was actually as scared of him as he is of the monster . . .

Back in Monstropolis, only the finest monsters were chosen for the risky job of collecting children's screams. Although children were strange and considered dangerous, monsters needed children's screams of fright to provide power to their city.

Once in a while, a monster slipped up, and a human item—a stray sock or toy—made its way into Monstropolis. When that happened, everyone rushed to decontaminate the entire area, including the monster.

Then, one day, the unthinkable happened—a human child made her way into Monstropolis!

It happened when a monster named Sulley encountered a child who wasn't scared of him. In fact, she giggled when she saw him and called him "Kitty!" She followed Sulley back through the door between their two worlds. Sulley was terrified. Who knew what chaos a loose child could cause in Monstropolis?

However, it didn't take long for Sulley to realize that the girl wasn't as scary as he had thought. In fact, she was sort of . . . cute. Nice. Even lovable. He even gave her a name—Boo.

Although they were very different, Sulley and Boo became friends. Then, Sulley's boss asked him to demonstrate how to scare children. Sulley entered a fake bedroom and leaped with a wild *ROARRRRR!*

He didn't realize that Boo was watching. She whimpered with fear. Maybe Sulley wasn't so nice, after all! He was so scary, so different. . . .

But Sulley reassured her. "Boo, it's me!" he told her gently. Even though he had roared like a scary monster, he was still her friend.

Sulley proved it by working with his friend Mike to make sure Boo made it home safely. Later, he led her back into her own bedroom. He tucked her into bed with her favorite teddy bear.

"Nothing's coming out of the closet to scare you anymore. Right?" he said.

Boo smiled. "Kitty!" she said happily.

Sulley was happy, too. He had learned that children were not scary, and he had even saved Monsters, Inc., by discovering that laughter was more powerful than screams.

Playing Along

from *The Lion King II: Simba's Pride*

Always make time for fun.

Simba's daughter Kiara knew all about having fun. She loved to stalk butterflies on the Pride Lands and play with her friends Timon and Pumbaa.

One day, Kiara sneaked away from Pride Rock to explore a new part of the Pride Lands. Suddenly, she slipped down a hill and—WHAM!—crashed into another lion cub!

His name was Kovu, and he was an Outsider. But Kiara didn't care about that. She and Kovu played tag and had fun until Simba showed up and chased Kovu away.

As Kovu grew up in the Outlands, he slowly forgot about having fun. All he could think about was what his leader, Zira, taught him. She told him that Simba and his family were the enemy, and Kovu's destiny was to destroy them and take over the Pride Lands.

One day, Zira sent Kovu to find Kiara. Kiara was happy to see her old friend. The two of them went hunting on the savanna. There, they found Timon and Pumbaa trying to scare some hungry birds away from the bugs they wanted to eat.

"Shoo!" Timon cried. "Go on, shoo!" He turned to Kovu. "You want to lend a voice?" he asked. "*Grr. Grr. Roar!* Work with me."

"Like this," Kiara added. "*ROOOOOAAAR!*"

The birds leaped up, startled. Kovu roared, too. More birds flapped into the air.

They began chasing the birds. "Why are we doing this?" Kovu asked.

"This is just for fun," said Kiara, laughing.

Fun? Kovu started to remember a little bit about having fun. . . .

The foursome chased the birds into a canyon. Suddenly, they heard an annoyed snort. They had run right into a herd of rhinos!

"Uh-oh!" Kiara cried.

"I hate rhinos!" Timon screamed.

They turned and ran as fast as they could in the other direction. Kovu laughed as he ran. This was fun!

When they were safe from the rhinos, the four friends collapsed. "You're okay, kid," Timon told Kovu.

Kovu wasn't sure what to say. All he knew was that, for a few minutes, he had forgotten all about Zira's mission, and taking over the Pride Lands, and his difficult life in the Outlands.

He had been too busy having fun.

The Other Side

from *Lady and the Tramp II: Scamp's Adventure*

Sometimes it takes leaving to appreciate what you've left behind.

Through the fence in his backyard, Scamp spied a group of wild dogs tussling with the dogcatcher.

Now that was the life for him! He didn't belong in a house with a family. He was a wild dog at heart and there was no denying it. Scamp daydreamed about life on the other side of the fence. No baths, no leash, no rules. What could be better?

That night, determined to run away, Scamp pulled himself free and raced down the dark street. He turned the corner and came upon Angel, a pretty little dog from the group he had seen earlier. The two became fast friends. Angel took Scamp back to the junkyard where the other wild dogs were.

The Junkyard Dogs were a rough crowd, and they didn't take to strangers quickly. "Hey, collar boy! How's life on the end of a chain?" they jeered at Scamp.

"I've had enough of the house dog life! I want to be wild and free just like you guys!" Scamp assured them.

The next night, Angel and Scamp went off walking along the train tracks together. "What are you doing out here?" Angel asked. "Don't you have a nice family back home?"

Scamp explained that having a family meant taking baths, eating out of bowls, and sleeping in a bed. Who would want that?

Angel confessed that she would. She longed to be adopted. "The Junkyard Dogs aren't much of a family. But what choice do I have?" she said sadly.

"What more do you need?" Scamp asked. He didn't see that the wild life had its downside, too.

Just then, as the dogs crossed a railroad bridge, a train came barreling down the tracks behind them.

"Run!" yelled Angel.

Scamp raced down the rails. This was just the kind of excitement he had been looking for! But as he neared safety, his paw got stuck in the tracks. Angel ran back for him and, seconds before the train passed over them, they crashed through the railroad ties into the river below.

They finally found each other on the riverbank, both lucky to have survived. The world away from home was more dangerous than Scamp had imagined. Scamp was beginning to realize that maybe junkyard life wasn't all fun and games.

Scamp and Angel continued walking and, after a little while, they ended up in Scamp's old neighborhood. Scamp decided to take a peek in his family's window. He was surprised by what he saw. Everyone looked sad and worried. They had spent the whole day searching for him.

"Gosh, I didn't think they'd miss me that much," said Scamp, feeling very guilty.

"You didn't think they'd miss you? I can't believe you'd run away from a home like this," said Angel in shocked disbelief. "I'd give anything to have what you have."

Scamp had never thought about what he did have. He was always too busy thinking about what he *didn't* have. Maybe his old life wasn't so bad, after all. Scamp wasn't ready to go back yet, but he was starting to think that Angel had a point.

The Skating Lesson

from *Beauty and the Beast: The Enchanted Christmas*

———⧜———

Love has a better chance of finding you if you are open to it.

"Voilà! There he is!" Lumiere, the candelabrum, exclaimed. The enchanted objects inside the Beast's castle had been searching for the Master for quite a while. Finally, Lumiere peered out a window and spotted him outside. "No time to waste!" he said to Cogsworth, the mantel clock, Mrs. Potts, the teapot, and Chip, the teacup, as he led them down a hallway, now on the lookout for Belle. "We must find a way to get them together."

It was the day before Christmas, but the holiday was the last thing on anyone's mind. Instead, the entire household was plotting to get Belle and the Beast to fall in love. Then the spell over the castle would be broken; the Beast and the objects would regain their human forms, and they would all live happily ever after.

Farther down the hall, the objects found Belle. Lumiere grabbed her hand and began pulling her outside.

"A wonderful day for a morning constitutional," he pointed out.

"Yeah, yeah!" added Chip. "Or you could go ice-skating! Let's go!" They were hoping that Belle would run into the Beast, and the two would spend some time together.

Belle grabbed her coat and ice skates, and soon she was outside on the frozen pond, skating and twirling around.

"Ha-ha! You were right!" Belle exclaimed as the objects watched and waved at her from the snowy bank. "This is a perfect day for skating!"

Belle was so busy enjoying herself that she did not see the Beast, grumpily lumbering over to her. "What is the meaning of this?" he boomed just as Belle skated past him.

Belle was so startled that she lost her footing and fell onto the ice.

The Beast had no patience for silly activities such as ice-skating. He reached down, lifted Belle roughly by the collar, and set her on her feet. "You should be more careful!" he scolded. Then he turned and started toward the castle—only to slip and fall himself.

Belle smiled and skated a graceful circle around him. "I'll try to remember that," she said, teasing the Beast. He grumbled and tried to stand up, but fell again. "You should be more careful!" Belle said, giving the

Beast a dose of his own medicine. Then she offered him a hand.

"I can do it by myself!" the Beast snapped. But trying once more to stand up, he fell for a third time.

Belle skated behind him and helped him up. "Come on," she said gently. "You'll never get there until you learn to skate. It's easy. Watch." Belle demonstrated how to push off and glide across the ice. "Now you try it," she said to the Beast.

The Beast wasn't wearing ice skates, but he slid his feet across the ice, concentrating hard and trying to keep his balance. He grew more and more confident with each sliding step. "I think I've got it!" he said at last. The Beast moved in a circle around Belle. "Ha-ha-ha! This is easy!" he exclaimed.

Then he grabbed Belle's hands. And as they twirled together on the frozen ice, the Beast's cold, hard heart began to warm. He had opened himself up to learning something new. But it seemed a little bit of love had sneaked in, too.

A New View for Neera

from *Dinosaur*

The old way is not the only way.

ladar had just joined the herd of dinosaurs traveling to the Nesting Grounds. The group was moving at a fast pace, and the older dinosaurs were very afraid of being left behind. Aladar saw no reason why the group shouldn't stick together and help the weaker ones along. But when he asked Kron, their heartless leader, about slowing down, Kron told him to be quiet and mind his own business.

Before long, the herd reached a lake bed that was completely dry. "What do you want us to do?" asked Bruton, Kron's lieutenant. "Keep moving!" Kron ordered.

The older dinosaurs tried to keep up as Kron mercilessly drove the herd on. They hadn't had even a sip of water in days.

Kron's sister, Neera, cautioned him. "We've never gone this long without water. If we keep moving, we'll lose half the herd."

"Then we save the half that deserves to live," Kron replied coldly.

Neera nodded. She knew it was the way the herd had always lived. Every dinosaur for himself. Only the strong survive. These were the only rules the dinosaurs knew. Aladar was the first dinosaur to suggest that there could be another way.

When the herd finally found a little water, the young dinosaurs

pushed and shoved
to get their share.
But Aladar stopped
to help an older
dinosaur drink.

Neera had been
watching him.
"Why did you help
that old one?" she
asked.

"What else could
we do? Leave her behind?" Aladar said.

Neera seemed to think this was a fine idea. "It happens a lot," she
explained. "You don't survive if you're not—"

"Strong enough,"
Aladar finished for
her. "Is that you
talking, or your
brother?" he asked.

"Everything is so
different, I don't
know what to think
anymore," Neera

confessed. She had never heard ideas like Aladar's before.

"Neera, if we help each other, we *all* might make it to your Nesting
Grounds," Aladar told her.

But despite Aladar's hopes, the herd did not remain together.

Aladar stayed behind to help the older dinosaurs, and Neera pushed ahead with Kron. But Neera hadn't forgotten Aladar's words. As the herd labored to reach the Nesting Grounds, other dinosaurs became tired and weak. Neera saw two exhausted orphan dinosaurs falling behind.

She went back to them. "It's okay, little ones," Neera said. She nudged one of the orphans back to his feet. "We're going to make it," she reassured them. She stayed behind to walk slowly with the scared young dinosaurs.

Neera had never allowed herself to feel for the weaker ones before. But now that Aladar had opened her heart to another way, there was no going back. She looked behind her, searching for a sign of Aladar and the old ones in the distance. She hoped they would make it.

Word Power

from *Atlantis: The Lost Empire*

Reading unlocks many wonders.

Ever since discovering the lost city of Atlantis, Milo Thatch had been eager to learn everything he could about it. He questioned Kida, the king's daughter, asking her all about her world.

Kida had questions for Milo, too. "How is it you found your way to this place?" she asked.

"It wasn't easy," Milo replied. "If it weren't for this book, we never would have made it." He held up *The Shepherd's Journal*, which he had translated and used to guide the expedition to Atlantis.

Kida turned the journal over in her hands. She ran her fingers over the pages, then looked at Milo.

"You mean you can understand this?" she asked.

"Yes," Milo said. "I'm a linguist—that's what I do. I can read Atlantean just like you."

Kida stared at him blankly.

Suddenly, Milo realized the truth. "You can't read, can you?" he blurted out.

"No one can," Kida replied. "Such knowledge has been lost to us."

Kida looked at the book again. Then she grabbed Milo.

"Here," she said. "Let me show you something." She pulled back a tarp, revealing a giant stone fish.

"It looks like some sort of vehicle," Milo said.

"Yes, but no matter what I try, it will not respond," Kida told him.

Milo studied the writing carved on the fish. It gave directions for starting the vehicle. As he read them aloud, Kida followed the instructions. Within moments, the vehicle sprang to life and hovered above the ground!

After that, Kida was eager to show Milo the wonders of her home. Milo was amazed at the culture of Atlantis. At the end of the tour, Kida led Milo to the edge of a pond.

"You know, Kida," Milo said, "the most we ever hoped to find were some crumbling buildings, maybe some broken pottery. Instead, we found a living, thriving society."

Kida shook her head sadly. "True, our people live," she said, "but our culture is dying."

"I don't know what you mean," Milo said.

"I have brought you to this place to ask for your help," Kida said. "There is a mural here with writing all around the pictures." She led him down to the water's edge. They swam to a wall filled with murals. She wanted to know if anything written there would help Atlantis regain the knowledge it had lost.

Milo was excited. "This is amazing!" he said. "A complete history of Atlantis!"

He was grateful for all the years he'd spent studying languages. His knowledge of words had helped him find Atlantis, and now it would enable him to unlock the lost world's fascinating secrets.

Do the Right Thing

Stories About Integrity

An Honorable Outlaw

from *Robin Hood*

When right is on your side, you can't go wrong.

It seemed that things could not get any worse in Nottingham. Ever since good King Richard had left on his travels, his wicked brother, Prince John, had been making life miserable for everyone. He had doubled and even tripled the taxes, and the poor folks who could not afford to pay them were thrown into the castle jail!

Luckily, Robin Hood kept the people's hopes alive. One night, he and Little John sneaked into the castle. They managed to take the jail keys from the sleeping Sheriff of Nottingham.

"It can't be!" said Friar Tuck when he saw Little John sneak into the jail cell.

"Shhhh," Little John whispered. "Quiet. We're bustin' out of here."

While Little John freed the

prisoners, Robin Hood climbed up into Prince John's bedchamber. There he found the prince asleep in his bed, his adviser, Sir Hiss, asleep in his own, and next to them, the many bags of gold that they had collected in unfair taxes.

Silently, Robin Hood rigged a pulley system so that, one by one, he could pass the bags of gold down to Little John in the courtyard. But just as Robin Hood was leaving with the last two bags, Sir Hiss awoke! He lunged after the bags, grabbing hold of one of them with his teeth and breaking it open. The noise of the falling coins woke the prince.

"Guards, my gold!" Prince John shouted, raising the alarm.

But Robin Hood was already out the window, climbing down the pulley line. He caught up with Little John and the townsfolk. They loaded the gold onto a cart and, with the Sheriff and the guards in pursuit, they made a break for the drawbridge.

"Wait for me!" little Tagalong the rabbit called out after them. He had fallen behind the others and was chasing after the cart. Robin Hood turned back for him, just managing to pick up Tagalong and race away before the guards caught up to them. But when Robin Hood and Tagalong got to the drawbridge, the front gate was closed. Little John and the others were waiting on the other side.

Through one of the holes in the gate, Robin Hood passed tiny Tagalong to Little John.

"Keep going," Robin Hood said to them. "Don't worry about me."

So, as Little John led the others to safety in Sherwood Forest, Robin Hood stayed behind. He climbed up the gate, then jumped and, grabbing hold of a rope, swung over the heads of the approaching guards.

After a long chase, the Sheriff finally had Robin Hood cornered in the castle tower.

"This time we got him, for sure," the Sheriff said with a sneer as he chased Robin Hood up the tower stairs. Then, reaching the tower room, the Sheriff used a torch to set the curtains on fire. The flames rapidly spread, forcing Robin Hood to jump into the castle moat far below. He easily swam to safety on the far shore.

Prince John and Sir Hiss watched in disbelief as Robin Hood got away—and as the castle continued to burn.

And soon they had even bigger problems. Good King Richard returned from his travels, and Prince John, Sir Hiss, and the Sheriff of Nottingham were all sentenced to work in the Royal Rock Pile for their misdeeds.

As for Robin Hood, King Richard was grateful to him for looking after the people. He knew that Robin Hood always fought for fairness and justice—even if he *was* an outlaw.

Jane's Big Mistake

from *Peter Pan in Return to Never Land*

Don't let your anger lead you to do the wrong thing.

Peter Pan had just saved Jane from Captain Hook, who had kidnapped her right out of her London bedroom. Peter then took Jane to the Lost Boys' hideout. Jane had heard all about Never Land and Peter Pan and the Lost Boys from her mother, Wendy. But she had stopped believing. Now she realized that they were real! But Jane was a serious girl. It didn't take long before she got tired of the boys' childish games and pranks. She didn't have time for fun. She had to get home.

"The only way out of here is to fly," Peter Pan told her.

Jane tried to fly, but she wasn't very good at it. On her final attempt, when she fell to the ground, her special notebook tumbled out of her pocket.

"Hey, what's this?" asked Peter as he picked it up.

"Oh, give it back. It's my list of things to do, places to be—important things," said Jane.

Peter didn't think any of that sounded like fun. "Keep away from Jane!" he cried. The Lost Boys began tossing the notebook around.

"Give it back!" Jane yelled. "Stop it! This isn't funny!"

But the Lost Boys just laughed. They kept at it until Cubby accidentally swallowed the notebook whole. Jane was furious. Peter tried to apologize, but Jane was too mad to listen.

"Oh, grow up! You're just a bunch of ridiculous children!" she yelled. And with that, Jane stomped off into the woods by herself.

Captain Hook had been waiting for a chance to use Jane to get to Peter Pan. He sat down near Jane in the woods and began to sob loudly. He was a surprisingly good actor. He managed to convince Jane that all he wanted to do was to leave the island and return to his home, just like she did.

"But blast it all," he told her, "Peter stole my treasure, and my men would mutiny if I so much as tried to leave without it." Hook continued, "I'll give you passage home on my ship, and you can help me recover my treasure! The treasure is useless to Peter. He's not sensible like you and me. He's just a boy who'll never grow up."

Hook's words stirred up all of the anger Jane had felt before. She forgot that Hook was not trustworthy and accepted his proposal. He gave her a whistle to blow once she found the treasure.

Jane left Captain Hook and soon came upon Peter and the Lost

Boys. Jane felt funny about tricking them, but she still hadn't forgotten their teasing. "Why don't we play a game?" Jane suggested. "Like maybe . . . Treasure Hunt?"

Peter agreed, on the condition that Jane try both to think like a Lost Boy and have fun like a Lost Boy. Before Jane knew it, that was exactly what she was doing. Peter showed her all around the island. It was wonderful! She soon forgot all about being angry.

Then, Jane peeked into a small cave. "The treasure! I found—" she started to say, but then she remembered her deal with Hook. Immediately, she realized she had made a mistake. She had let anger and frustration cloud her judgment. Peter Pan and the Lost Boys were her friends. She couldn't betray them. Jane took the whistle out of her pocket and threw it into the water.

Brave Through and Through

from *Aladdin: The Return of Jafar*

Always stand up for what you know is right.

Iago the parrot had always known how to look out for bird number one—himself. That had once meant buddying up to Jafar, the evil palace vizier. However, things had changed. Jafar was trapped as a genie in a lamp, and Iago was trapped right along with him.

Finally, Iago escaped from the lamp. He was going to release Jafar, too, but he thought better of it. Maybe it would be safer and easier to be out on his own.

He flew to Agrabah, reaching the palace just in time to see Aladdin arrive to visit Princess Jasmine. Rajah seemed especially happy to see Aladdin.

Iago hid and listened to Aladdin and Jasmine talk. He could hardly believe what they were saying.

"The street rat is living in the palace now?" Iago exclaimed. Then he realized this was his chance. "The kid is my

ticket back into power!" He was so excited that he hugged a palace pigeon.

At first, Iago's plans didn't go well. Aladdin was ready to turn him over to the Sultan. Then, some bandits appeared and started chasing Aladdin. Iago tried to escape, but ended up accidentally saving Aladdin from the bandits instead.

"Thanks for your help," Aladdin told Iago. "You saved me."

The Sultan and Jasmine were furious about Iago's return. But Aladdin convinced them to allow the bird to live.

Iago was surprised at the brave way Aladdin had stood up for him. "Nobody's ever looked out for me before," he murmured. "Now it's like I owe *him*."

The Genie overheard and morphed into Jiminy Cricket. "Just let your conscience be your guide!" he chirped.

"Conscience?" Iago replied. "Never had one. Never."

Meanwhile, Jafar escaped from the lamp and started plotting his revenge against Aladdin. He forced Iago to help him, reminding the bird that he'd always been a villain through and through.

Iago was too fearful to resist. With the parrot's help, Jafar captured the Sultan, Jasmine, and the Genie. Then he magically turned himself into the spitting image

of Jasmine. He went to the palace and accused Aladdin of murdering the Sultan, ordering the guards to execute him.

Iago felt guilty. He knew he should help Aladdin, but he feared Jafar's wrath. Finally he worked up the courage to do the right thing. He freed the Genie, who then saved Aladdin from the guards.

Iago had paid back his debt to Aladdin. But he'd also realized he was braver than he'd thought.

When Jafar turned Agrabah into a pit of lava, Iago considered flying away. That was what the old Iago would have done.

But this Iago was bolder and braver. Instead of leaving, he helped Aladdin defeat Jafar.

Iago finally learned that looking out for bird number one didn't have to mean being a cowardly villain. It could also mean standing up for his friends—and for himself.

Making Peace

from *Pocahontas II: Journey to a New World*

Choose reason over rage. Violence is not the answer.

ll of the settlers in Jamestown gathered around the dock to greet the ship arriving from England. John Rolfe and his crew had sailed all the way across the ocean at the command of King James to resolve tensions between the settlers and the natives.

The Indian princess Pocahontas stood among the crowd, watching as the ship's cargo was unloaded. In the nearby woods, her people, hidden and armed, were quietly watching, too.

As Rolfe rode his horse down the gangplank, another settler from the ship made his way through the crowd. He carried a heavy pack on his shoulder and bumped Pocahontas roughly as he walked by. "Filthy barbarian," he grunted as he passed her.

Just then, Rolfe's horse panicked. It reared up, threw Rolfe to the ground, and began galloping dangerously through the crowd. The settler who had insulted Pocahontas was picking some coins off the ground, with his back turned to the charging horse. The horse was about to trample him! Pocahontas dove toward him, knocking the settler out of the way a second before the horse thundered by.

The settler never saw the horse. He was furious about being pushed aside. "Bloody savage!" he cried, raising his hand to strike Pocahontas.

Immediately, the natives in the woods revealed themselves and drew their bows. The startled settlers saw them and raised their muskets. A battle was about to erupt. Without thinking of her own safety, Pocahontas quickly ran and stood between the two sides. "No, wait!" she called out, raising her arms.

Pocahontas knew it was wrong to fight all of the settlers because of the bad behavior of a single man. It would only lead to greater anger and more bloodshed. Her people lowered their weapons. Rolfe raised his hand, and the settlers lowered their arms, too.

That evening, Rolfe went to the tribal village to meet with the chief. He stood before Chief Powhatan and spoke, as the rest of the tribe listened. He explained his mission.

"To build trust, I would like you to sail back with me . . . to meet my king," Rolfe said.

"I don't want the pale chief's land. He wants mine. Why doesn't he cross the Salt Water to see me?" Powhatan replied.

The tribe's resentment began to swell. "Your kind are barbarians," one of the natives jeered at Rolfe. "They want our land. They mean to—"

But Pocahontas interrupted him. "Is that what they want?" she questioned.

There was too much at stake to jump to conclusions. They couldn't allow anger to cloud their judgment. They needed to know the facts if the fighting was ever to stop. "Father," Pocahontas said, turning to Powhatan, "someone must go." She volunteered herself.

At first, the tribe thought Pocahontas was being disloyal and siding with the settlers. But Powhatan saw the wisdom of Pocahontas's position. In order for there to be peace, she should try to talk with the British king. Maybe, if the two sides could understand each other, the fighting could end for good. It was decided that Pocahontas would sail to England to meet King James. The fate of her people, and of Jamestown, was in her hands.

Max and the Map

from *A Goofy Movie*

Lying will lead you in the wrong direction.

So far, Max had spent his entire trip to Lake Destiny moping and complaining. But that morning, his dad, Goofy, had an idea about how to get Max more engaged.

"Seems to me you need to start taking some responsibility around here," Goofy said in a mock serious tone. Then he stood up and tapped Max on each shoulder with the road map.

"I, Goofy, hereby dub my son Maximillian 'Official Navigator and Head Which-Wayer' of this here road trip!" he said.

"Seriously?" asked Max.

"I'm not even looking at the map anymore. As a matter of fact, you can pick all the stops from here to Lake Destiny. I trust ya wholeheartedly, son," Goofy assured him.

Max guiltily took the map from his dad. Little did Goofy know that Max had secretly taken charge of navigating the night before. He had erased Goofy's line directing them to Lake Destiny, and drawn in a new one leading them to Los Angeles. Max desperately wanted to get to L.A. so he could go to the Powerline concert. It was the only way he was ever going to impress Roxanne, the girl he really liked.

At their hotel that night, Goofy and Max ran into their friends Pete and his son P.J. Max quietly told P.J. about what he had done. Max had thought the coast was clear, but Pete overheard their whole conversation.

"I hate to be the bearer of bad news," Pete later told Goofy, "but I heard the little mutant telling P.J. that he changed the map, so . . . you're headin' straight to L.A., pal."

Goofy knew Max had been distant lately, but he never thought his son would *lie* to him. Then he looked at the map. Pete was right . . . and Goofy was heartbroken.

The next day, still hoping that Max would come around, Goofy played it cool. As they approached a junction, he turned to Max. "Well, here ya go, navigator. Just follow my route on the map," he said.

Max was trying to work up the nerve to trick his father, but it was harder than he thought. "Okay . . . umm . . . well . . . " He stalled.

"C'mon, Max!" Goofy said.

"Go . . . rrr . . . left!" Max yelled, choosing the direction of L.A. Goofy swerved off the road onto a scenic canyon overlook.

Max had never seen his father so angry. He started to confess about the directions, when their car began to roll downhill. Goofy and Max jumped inside and tried to hit the brakes, but before they could, the car crashed through the guardrail and fell hard into the water below.

As they floated down the river, Goofy let Max have it. Max knew it was wrong to lie and he apologized. But he also explained that Goofy never thought about what *he* wanted to do. After all, Max wasn't a little kid anymore.

"No matter how big you get, you'll always be my son," Goofy told him. As he said the words, Goofy and Max stopped arguing. Sometimes it was hard, but being honest and open was worth it. Max realized that nothing—not even Roxanne—would make him risk his dad's trust again.

Tiggers, Where Are You?

from *The Tigger Movie*

Act kindly, even if it means getting stung.

"Halloo! Tigger's family!" Tigger called out as he peered up into the trees.

Tigger's friends were standing nearby. "I didn't know Tigger had a family," Piglet said.

"Oh, yes," Pooh replied. "Only it appears that he has lost them."

"He seems to be looking for them," Eeyore added.

"Is that something we should be doing, too?" asked Piglet.

They decided that it was. If Tigger was on a search, surely they should take some time to help him.

So Piglet, Pooh, and Eeyore began wandering all over the Hundred-Acre Wood. "Tigger's family?" they called, looking under rocks and into bushes.

Soon Eeyore, who had walked to a nearby pond, called Piglet and Pooh over. "I found them. Bouncin' like anything. Stripes and all," Eeyore said.

The creatures Eeyore found did indeed bounce. And they had stripes, too. But they weren't tiggers. They were frogs!

"Do these particular tiggers seem rather strange to you, Piglet?" Pooh asked.

"Yes," Piglet admitted. "Still, I suppose you never can tell with tiggers," he added.

So, they decided to invite some of the frogs over to Tigger's house. "We need your help. It would just take a minute," Pooh explained to the frogs. But the frogs wouldn't listen. "Bother," said Pooh.

Piglet tried his best, too. "Nice tigger," he said softly, as he reached to pick one up. But the frog jumped right out of his hand.

"I don't remember tiggers being quite this slippery," Piglet said.

"I don't remember a tigger making quite that sort of sound, either," said Pooh. "I don't think these are the right tiggers, after all."

The friends decided to keep looking. Soon they came upon a big tree. Pooh thought the tree looked like a bee sort of tree. And that meant honey.

"Do you think it could be Tigger's family up there, Pooh Bear?" asked Piglet.

"I suppose there's only one way to find out," said Pooh as he climbed up the tree.

Pooh was right about there being honey up in the tree. He tried to sneak a little smackerel, but he got stung by the bees. To get to the honey more easily, Pooh sang the bees to sleep with a soft lullaby.

Piglet and Eeyore began to wonder what was taking Pooh so long. Piglet climbed up the tree to check.

"Pooh Bear, are you stuck?" Piglet asked when he reached the beehive.

The question surprised Pooh. He fell into the hive and woke up the bees. The bees were not pleased to find a honey thief in their home. They chased after Pooh and Piglet as the two friends tumbled out of the tree.

"I have come to the conclusion," Pooh said as he, Piglet, and Eeyore ran away from the angry bees, "that these bees are not the right sort of tiggers."

It looked like finding Tigger's family wouldn't be so easy, after all. But there were lots of other trees to check in the Hundred-Acre Wood. Pooh and his friends would just have to try again tomorrow, because that's what you did when you wanted your friend to be happy.

Aladar's Stand

from *Dinosaur*

One strong voice can inspire many.

If it hadn't been for Aladar's encouragement, Baylene and Eema would have given up. The two older dinosaurs had fallen behind the herd on their difficult journey to the Nesting Grounds. Aladar stayed with them. After narrowly escaping a nasty carnotaur, the small group finally reached their destination.

"I don't get it," Aladar said as they drank from the lake. "Where's the rest of the herd?"

Aladar couldn't figure out how he and Baylene and Eema could have gotten ahead of the faster and stronger dinosaurs. Then Eema realized that they had entered the Nesting Grounds from a different direction than usual.

"That's the way we used to get in here," she told Aladar, indicating what had once been a mountain pass, but was now a steep wall of rock. Eema shook her head. "The others will never make it over that," she said.

Aladar knew that the carnotaur they had just escaped was close behind. If the herd tried to get over those rocks, they would never make it to safety in time. Aladar bravely ran off to warn the others.

When Aladar finally found the herd, Kron was driving the dinosaurs up the rocks that blocked the mountain pass.

"Get the herd out of here! A carnotaur's coming!" Aladar cried.

Kron ignored him. "Keep moving!" he barked.

"Stop!" Aladar yelled.

"There's a safer way! You can't get over the rocks. There's a sheer drop on the other side. You're going to kill the herd!"

But still Kron refused to listen.

Moments later, the dinosaurs heard a carnotaur roar. "He's led that monster right to us! This way!" Kron yelled as he turned to scramble up the rock wall. The dinosaurs moved to follow him.

"No! Don't move!" cried Aladar. "If we scatter, he'll pick us off! Stand together!"

As the carnotaur approached the herd, Aladar roared. Then, one by one, except for Kron, the entire herd lifted up their heads and joined him, bellowing loudly at the carnotaur. It worked! The carnotaur was frightened by the noise and started to back away. But then it spotted Kron alone on the rocks. The carnotaur charged. Aladar raced to defend Kron, but he was too late. Kron had already met his end at the hands of the carnotaur. Aladar battled the ferocious dinosaur until it plummeted off the rocks to its death.

The herd realized that Aladar's courage and compassion had helped them survive and arrive safely at the Nesting Grounds. They had found their new leader.

Jane Saves the Day

from *Peter Pan in Return to Never Land*

Do your best to fix your mistakes.

Tweeeee! Tootles the Lost Boy blew his new whistle. "No, wait!" cried Jane, but it was too late. Captain Hook and his pirates were already upon them.

"Ha-ha! The treasure is ours!" Hook cried gleefully, as he grabbed Peter Pan. "It's time for you to meet your Maker!"

Jane never should have made that deal with Hook! Hook had told her that all she had to do was find his treasure, then blow a whistle, and he would come to take her home. But then Jane realized she couldn't betray Peter and the Lost Boys. Jane had thrown the whistle away, but Tootles had found it.

Peter quickly figured out what Jane had done. He was shocked. "You're a traitor, Jane!" he cried as Hook's pirates dragged him and the Lost Boys away.

"No, Peter, I'll save you. I will!" Jane called out. Hook had promised Jane that he wouldn't hurt Peter and the Lost Boys, but she had been a fool to trust him. Jane knew she had gotten her friends into this mess. Now it was up to her to get them out of it.

Jane ran to see if Tinker Bell the fairy could help her save Peter Pan and the Lost Boys. But Tinker Bell was very weak. Her light was fading because Jane had said she didn't believe in fairies. Now Jane knelt beside Tink and tried very hard to believe. Slowly, Tinker Bell's light began to shine brighter and brighter. In a short while, she was as good as new.

Then, Tink and Jane raced to Hook's ship. Hook had chained Peter to an anchor so he couldn't fly away. "Say your prayers, Peter Pan!" Hook said with a snarl.

"Not so fast, you old codfish! Or you'll have to answer to me!" cried Jane as she and Tink stormed the ship. The Lost Boys cheered.

"Jane!" cried Peter, looking up in surprise.

Jane swiped a dagger from one of the pirates and cut the ropes binding the boys. Then the boys used their slingshots to shoot jewels out into the water. Hook's pirates were so greedy that they jumped overboard after the loot.

In the meantime, Tink had set to work trying to get the keys to Peter's chains from around Hook's neck. Hook's assistant, Smee, swung an oar at Tink, but ended up knocking out Hook instead. Jane darted over and grabbed the keys just as Hook came to his senses.

"Give it up, girl!" he yelled as he chased Jane. But Jane made it to Peter and unlocked his chains. Now Hook didn't stand a chance! As Hook swung down toward them on a rope, Peter threw his dagger at the rope holding Captain Hook, slicing it in two.

Then, Hook fell into the water—just escaping a hungry octopus. Luckily, the other pirates rescued him.

Peter and the Lost Boys were saved. Jane might have made a mistake, but she had worked hard to right it, and that was what really counted.

One Lucky Llama

from *The Emperor's New Groove*

Even though you may have been wronged in the past, you've got to keep doing right.

ne day, the selfish and spoiled Emperor Kuzco called a kind peasant named Pacha to appear before him. He began asking Pacha questions about his village. Pacha told the Emperor that his family had lived on the same hilltop for generations. They all loved it there.

Kuzco was pleased. "I just needed an insider's opinion before I okayed the spot for my pool," he said.

"What . . .? I don't understand. . . ." Pacha was confused.

Kuzco explained that he planned to destroy Pacha's village in order to build a vacation home, humbly named Kuzcotopia, on the same hilltop.

"But . . . where will we live?" asked a worried Pacha.

"Hmm . . . don't know, don't care," said Kuzco with a shrug.

Pacha was devastated.

That night, when he returned home, he found an odd sack in his cart. He slowly opened the sack and, much to his surprise, a llama poked out its head.

"Where did you come from, little guy?" Pacha asked as he reached down to pet the animal.

"No touchy!" the llama exclaimed.

Pacha screamed. A llama that could talk? How could this be? Then the llama talked some more: "Oh, wait. I know you. You're that whiny peasant!"

Immediately, Pacha recognized the voice . . . Emperor Kuzco! As it turned out, Kuzco's evil adviser had fed him a potion in an attempt to kill the emperor, but ended up turning him into a llama instead. But Kuzco didn't know what had happened, and, of course, neither did Pacha.

Kuzco demanded that Pacha escort him back to the city.

"I can't let you go back unless you change your mind and build your summer home somewhere else," Pacha replied.

Kuzco flatly refused. "I don't make deals with peasants!" he huffed and stomped off into the jungle. Pacha tried to warn him that the jungle was a dangerous place for a llama who was actually an emperor who didn't know the way. Kuzco ignored him.

"Fine! Go ahead! If there's no Kuzco, there's no Kuzcotopia!"
Pacha said to himself.

Soon, Pacha started to feel guilty. He knew it was wrong to leave
Kuzco alone. Kuzco may have mistreated him, but Pacha still did not
want to see him hurt. Pacha set off into the jungle to follow Kuzco.

Sure enough, it didn't take long before Kuzco found himself in big
trouble: he had stumbled into a pack of sleeping jaguars and woken

them up! Kuzco ran as fast as he could, but the jaguars were faster. He was trapped on the edge of a steep cliff! But Pacha saw it all. He swung by on a vine and rescued Kuzco just in time.

Pacha was relieved. Even if Kuzco still planned on destroying his village, Pacha knew he had done the right thing.

Scamp Comes Home

from *Lady and the Tramp II: Scamp's Adventure*

---⚮---

It's never too late to say you're sorry.

"See that family?" Buster asked Scamp. "I want you to infiltrate their picnic and liberate their chicken . . . right out from under the nose of that meek little house dog."

"That family" happened to be Scamp's family, and "that house dog" was his father, Tramp. Scamp had run away from home to become a Junkyard Dog. Now, Buster was making Scamp prove he was Junkyard material.

"Come on, kid, you want to be wild and free, don't you? All it's gonna cost you is one juicy chicken," Buster said, taunting him.

More than anything, Scamp wanted to be a Junkyard Dog. But he didn't want to have to steal from his family to do it. His friend, Angel, tried to help him make the right decision. "You don't have to prove anything, Scamp. Just walk away!" she told him.

But Buster glared down at him, and Scamp ran toward the picnic

blanket. Scamp's family was so happy to see him. They had been very worried. But much to their disappointment, Scamp didn't stop. He tore through the picnic and snatched their chicken. "Scamp! Come back!" called Jim Dear as Scamp dodged Tramp and ran away.

Tramp chased after his son. Even though Scamp had put his family through an awful lot, all Tramp wanted was to have him home—safe

and sound. But Scamp thought he still belonged with the Junkyard Dogs, not his family. "I guess there are some things you have to learn on your own," Tramp told Scamp. "When you've had enough, our door is always open."

Scamp went back to join Buster and the gang, but he soon found out that Buster wasn't really his friend. That night when the dogcatcher came around, instead of helping Scamp, Buster stood by and let him get caught. Now Scamp was in the pound, and he was sure his family would never forgive him. He had made one mistake after another. Scamp was very sad.

Scamp should have known it would take more than a few mistakes—even big ones—to keep his dad away. Angel had seen Scamp get caught, and she ran to find Tramp. "You've got to come! Hurry! Scamp's in trouble!" she told him. Tramp didn't have to hear another word. He ran as fast as he could to the pound. It wasn't easy, but Tramp was able to rescue his frightened son.

As Scamp and Tramp walked home, Scamp guiltily turned to his father. "Pop," he said, "I'm so sorry. I shouldn't have run away."

Tramp nuzzled his son. And with relief, Scamp realized that everything would be okay. When Scamp saw the rest of his family waiting for him, he didn't have to ask—he knew they had forgiven him, too.

Go Your Own Way

from *Aladdin and the King of Thieves*

At some point, you have to stand on your own two feet.

 laddin watched as his father, Cassim, met Jasmine and the Sultan for the first time, and his heart filled with hope. Growing up, Aladdin hadn't known his father at all. Cassim had left his family to hunt for treasure as the leader of the Forty Thieves. But the mystical Oracle had helped Aladdin find his father in time for him to attend Aladdin and Jasmine's wedding. Now it seemed Cassim was turning over a new leaf.

All he needed was a second chance, Aladdin thought.

Aladdin did not know that Cassim had another motive for coming to the palace. He was after the Oracle, which Aladdin and Jasmine had received as a wedding gift. He could use the all-knowing Oracle to find the greatest treasure of all: the Hand of Midas.

On Aladdin's wedding day, Cassim found the palace treasure vault where the Oracle was stored. Iago, the parrot, handed him a set of lock picks.

"I promise you, bird," said Cassim, "after this, I go straight."

"Straight to the dungeon," said a surly voice behind Cassim. It was Rasoul, the captain of the palace guards. He and his men had caught the thieves red-handed. The guards brought Cassim and Iago before the Sultan, and they were sentenced to imprisonment in the dungeon . . . for life!

Aladdin was crushed. "I was so stupid to think I could change him," he said to the Genie that night.

Genie tried to comfort him. "Trying to show him a better life wasn't stupid, Al," he said.

But Aladdin just wished that his father had never come back into his life. Everything had been so perfect before he had shown up. Aladdin decided that the only way to return life to normal was to help his father to escape . . . then tell him to leave and never come back.

"I'm breaking my father out of that dungeon!" Aladdin said to Genie.

So, Aladdin dressed in his father's clothing, sneaked down to the dungeon, unlocked Cassim's shackles, then freed Iago.

"Why are you—?" Cassim said, puzzled by Aladdin's aid.

"We don't have much time," Aladdin interrupted. "While the guards chase me, you get out."

Aladdin's decoy plan worked. Aladdin, Cassim, and Iago were able to evade the guards—but not before Rasoul discovered that it was Aladdin who had freed the prisoners. The three of them raced out of the city, not stopping to talk until they were in the desert.

"They won't be able to pick up our trail till daylight," Cassim reassured Aladdin. "By then, we'll be long gone from Agrabah."

But Aladdin was turning to head back toward the palace. "I'm not going with you," he told his father. "I can't."

Cassim could not believe his ears. "Well, you can't go back," he said. "The moment they see your face, your life in Agrabah will be over!"

Iago agreed. "Kid, it's over. You're a criminal now," he said.

Nevertheless, Aladdin was determined to do the right thing, and he would not leave Jasmine. "I'm your son," he said to Cassim, "but I can't live your life."

With that, Aladdin rode back to the palace, prepared to face his punishment.

The Return of the Rightful King

from *The Lion King*

Use your power responsibly.

"The choice is yours, Scar," Simba said to his uncle. "Step down or fight."

After many years away from Pride Rock, Simba had returned to take his rightful place as king. Ever since Mufasa had died and Simba had run away, Scar and his allies, the hyenas, had ruled the kingdom—and they had ruled it badly. There was no food and no water. All the herds had begun leaving the Pride Lands, and Scar would do nothing to help them.

As the new king, Simba was going to change all that. But first he had to deal with Scar, and that would not be easy. Scar used one of his old tricks on Simba.

"If it weren't for you, Mufasa would still be alive!" Scar announced for all of the lionesses and hyenas to hear. "Do you deny it?"

Years before, Scar had tricked Simba into thinking that Mufasa's death had been his fault. Now he used the lie again to weaken Simba.

Simba could not deny Scar's charge.

"Then you're guilty!" Scar said accusingly as he moved toward Simba. Simba backed away, trying to rid his mind of the horrible memory of his father's death. In a flash, Simba's hind legs slipped off the edge of a cliff. He just managed to grab hold of the cliff ledge, but Scar loomed over him. Simba was at his uncle's mercy.

Scar looked into Simba's eyes, which were now wide with fear.
"Where have I seen this before?" Scar said quietly as Simba held on
for dear life. "Oh, yes! I remember! This is just the way your father
looked before he died." Then Scar leaned in and whispered in Simba's
ear: "And here's my little secret. *I killed Mufasa.*"

Wild with rage, Simba summoned every ounce of strength in his
body. He scrambled up the rock and leaped on top of Scar, pinning
him to the ground. Now it was Scar's eyes that showed fear.

"Tell them the truth," Simba told Scar, demanding that he share
his secret with everyone.

Scar had no choice. "I killed Mufasa," he admitted.

The truth was out, and the battle was on—because at that very
moment, the hyenas attacked Simba, knocking him off Scar. The

lionesses rushed to Simba's aid, attacking the hyenas. Soon Simba was able to fight his way clear of the hyenas and chase after Scar, who was retreating onto Pride Rock. Simba had him cornered.

"Simba, please," Scar pleaded, realizing that his fate was in Simba's hands. "Please, have mercy. I beg you."

"You don't deserve to live," Simba said, his eyes narrowing.

"It's the hyenas who are the real enemy," Scar argued. He told Simba that it had been the hyenas' idea to kill Mufasa.

Simba had no reason to believe Scar. Everything he had ever told Simba had been a lie. Scar was a murderer and he had betrayed his own family. And yet . . . Simba could not bring himself to kill him.

"I'm not like you," Simba said to Scar as he stepped aside to let Scar go. "Run. Run away, Scar, and never return."

Even in his fury, Simba did not allow his anger to turn him into a monster.

Woody the Star

from *Toy Story 2*

Never lose sight of what's truly important.

oody felt awful. Andy had accidentally ripped Woody's arm, which meant Woody had to stay home from Cowboy Camp. He watched sadly from the window as Andy left without him.

While Andy was gone, Woody mistakenly ended up at a yard sale. A man named Al grabbed him and took him back to his apartment. When Al left, Woody looked around for a way to escape. He had to get back to Andy!

Suddenly, a toy horse and a cowgirl doll popped into sight. "It's you!" the cowgirl cried. "It's really you!" A prospector doll waved from a box nearby.

Woody was confused. Why did they all seem to know him? The cowgirl, Jessie, showed him some magazines. Woody gasped. His picture was in them!

"You don't know

who you are, do you?" the Prospector asked.

Woody knew exactly who he was. He was Andy's favorite toy. But that wasn't what the Prospector meant. Bullseye the horse turned on the television.

"It's *Woody's Roundup!*" the TV announcer cried. "Starring Jessie the yodeling cowgirl . . . Stinky Pete the Prospector . . . Bullseye the horse . . . and Sher-r-riff Woody!"

Woody could hardly believe his eyes and ears. He was a star!

The other dolls showed Woody around the apartment. There were all kinds of shelves and cases filled with toys, games, books, and

clothes—all featuring Sheriff Woody. There was even a recording of his theme song! Woody felt great as he danced with his new friends.

They had to stop when Al returned to the apartment. He hurried straight toward Woody.

"Wait until the museum sees this Woody doll," he said eagerly. Then Al noticed Woody's ripped arm. "Oh, no!"

He called the Cleaner to come to repair Woody. The Cleaner carefully stitched Woody's arm back in place. Then he touched up Woody's paint job, covering over the name ANDY lettered on the bottom of Woody's foot.

After he left, the Prospector smiled. "You're a top-notch collectible now," he told Woody.

Woody wasn't sure he liked the sound of that. Even though being famous was fun, he knew he couldn't just forget about his old life. He liked his new friends, but he missed his old friends back home—especially Andy. He wouldn't rest until he found his way back home.

FAITH, TRUST, AND PIXIE DUST

STORIES ABOUT HOPE

A Silver Lining

from *Sleeping Beauty*

When all seems lost, a little hope makes a big difference.

It was a joyous day for King Stefan and the Queen. They had proclaimed a great holiday throughout the kingdom so that everyone might come to the castle to pay homage to their firstborn child, Princess Aurora.

Among the many guests that day were the three good fairies: Flora, Fauna, and Merryweather.

"The little darling," cooed Merryweather as the three fairies peeked inside little Aurora's cradle. The fairies had come to bestow gifts upon the princess; but each could give one, and only one.

Flora was the first to step forward to give her gift. She waved her wand over the child, saying, "Little princess, my gift shall be the gift of beauty."

Next, Fauna went to the cradle. "Tiny princess," she said, "my gift shall be the gift of song."

Last but not least, Merryweather flew to the baby's side. "Sweet princess, my gift shall be the—"

But Merryweather did not have a chance to finish. Just then, a cruel wind blew through the castle. Wispy flames appeared in the center of the great hall. The flames grew and grew—until out of the fire stepped the evil fairy, Maleficent.

"Well, quite a glittering assemblage, King Stefan," said Maleficent, looking around at all of the guests. "I really felt quite distressed at not receiving an invitation."

"You weren't wanted," replied Merryweather, red-faced and angry.

Maleficent pretended to be embarrassed, then said, "Well, in that event, I'd best be on my way." But before she left, Maleficent announced that she, too, had a gift to give the child. She raised her arms and struck her staff on the floor. "The princess shall indeed grow in grace and beauty, beloved by all who know her," she began. "But, before the sun sets on her sixteenth birthday, she shall prick her finger on the spindle of a spinning wheel . . . and die!"

The Queen gasped and picked up the baby. King Stefan ordered his guards to seize Maleficent. But in a flash of fire and smoke, she was gone.

King Stefan and the Queen were beside themselves with grief. But Flora reassured them: "Don't despair, Your Majesties. Merryweather still has her gift to give."

"Then, she can undo this fearful curse?" King Stefan asked.

"Oh, no, sire," said Merryweather sadly.

"Maleficent's powers are far too great," Flora added.

"But," said Fauna, "she can help." She turned to Merryweather and said, "Just do your best, dear."

Merryweather waved her wand, creating an image of a sixteen-year-old princess, lying on a bier. "Sweet princess," Merryweather began, "if through this wicked witch's trick, a spindle should your finger prick, a ray of hope there still may be in this gift I give to thee. Not in death, but just in sleep, the fateful prophecy you'll keep, and from this slumber you shall wake, when True Love's Kiss the spell shall break."

And so it was that Merryweather's gift was not only a gift to Aurora but to King Stefan, the Queen, and the entire kingdom. It was the gift of hope— hope that Maleficent's evil curse would someday be defeated.

Geppetto's Wish

from *Pinocchio*

———— ⬥ ————

Make a wish, it just may come true.

Long ago, on a clear night in a quaint little village, a kind, old wood-carver named Geppetto was putting the finishing touches on his newest handmade puppet.

"That makes a big difference!" Geppetto exclaimed as he painted a smile on the wooden face. "Now, I have just the name for you: Pinocchio!"

Geppetto turned on a music box and, using Pinocchio's strings,

danced him around the wood shop, as he introduced Pinocchio to his cat, Figaro, and his fish, Cleo. They all had great fun with Pinocchio, singing and dancing and laughing, until— *cuckoo, cuckoo*— Geppetto's many clocks struck the late hour. Then Geppetto climbed into bed and, as Figaro settled down to sleep next to him, the wood-carver stared across the room at Pinocchio.

"He almost looks alive!" said Geppetto. "Wouldn't it be nice if he were a real boy?"

Geppetto blinked his eyes and snuggled down into bed before he realized he had forgotten to open the window as he did every night at bedtime. Figaro, being closer, got up and opened it.

"Oh, Figaro, look!" Geppetto exclaimed, pointing at a dazzlingly bright star in the night sky. "The wishing star!" In an instant, Geppetto was out of bed and kneeling before the open window, wishing on the brilliant star.

Then, with his wish made, Geppetto confided in his cat. "I wished that my little Pinocchio might be a real boy!" he said. Geppetto climbed back into bed, saying to himself, "Just think. A real boy . . . a real boy . . ."

Soon, both he and Figaro were sleeping soundly—so soundly that they did not awaken when, in the stillness of the night, an amazing thing happened. A very bright light—as bright as a wishing star, perhaps—traveled through the open window and into the room.

Then, even more amazingly, the light took the shape of a beautiful fairy—the Blue Fairy. She stood over the sleeping Geppetto, saying, "You deserve to have your wish come true!" Silently, the Blue Fairy crossed the room, touched her wand to Pinocchio's head and said, "Little puppet made of pine, wake! The gift of life is thine!"

At that, a bright light emanated from the Blue Fairy's wand. When it faded, Pinocchio's eyes blinked, and he raised his hands to rub them.

"I can move!" Pinocchio exclaimed. He covered his mouth, surprised at the words that had come out. "I can talk!" he added with delight.

"Yes, Pinocchio," said the Blue Fairy. "I have given you life!" She advised Pinocchio to be good and to listen to his conscience, before she faded away like a dream and was gone.

A short time later, Pinocchio, still getting used to his legs, tripped over some paint pots. The noise woke Geppetto, who was amazed to find that his little wooden puppet was alive! At first, Geppetto was convinced he was still asleep, dreaming the whole thing. But there was the proof, walking and talking right in front of him. Before long, Geppetto began to believe his good fortune.

"It's—it's—my wish—" he realized, now overjoyed. "It's come true!"

A Magical Night

from *Cinderella*

It always seems darkest before the dawn.

inderella was excited. The Prince's ball was that night, and she was ready! Her mouse and bird friends had helped her sew a beautiful pink dress. It wasn't as fancy as the dresses her stepsisters, Anastasia and Drizella, were wearing, but it would do.

Cinderella went downstairs to show her stepfamily. "Do you like it?" she asked, twirling for them.

Drizella recognized the beads Cinderella wore. "Why, you little thief!" she cried, ripping them away. "My beads! Give them here!"

"And that's my sash!" Anastasia screeched.

Before long, they had ripped Cinderella's outfit to shreds. Then they left for the ball.

Cinderella was heartbroken. Her dream of attending the ball was ruined! Sobbing, she raced out of the house into the dark garden. She had never felt so alone, so hopeless and sad. Would she never know happiness again?

"It's just no use," she mumbled through her tears. "There's nothing left to believe in."

"Nothing?" a musical voice replied. "You don't really mean that."

Cinderella looked up and gasped. A smiling old woman had appeared out of nowhere!

"Now, dry those tears," the woman said cheerfully. "You can't go to the ball looking like that! Now, what in the world did I do with my magic wand?"

Cinderella could hardly believe it. The woman was her Fairy Godmother, and she was going to help Cinderella get to the ball after all!

The Fairy Godmother looked around and spotted a pumpkin.

"Now for the magic words," she said. She pronounced a lot of words Cinderella didn't recognize. And just like that, the pumpkin was magically transformed into an elegant coach.

Next, the Fairy Godmother created gleaming white horses, a footman, and a coachman. Finally, she turned to Cinderella.

"Good heavens, child," she exclaimed as she looked at her torn and tattered dress. "You can't go in that."

She waved her wand once more.

Cinderella felt the magic surround her. And when she looked down, the remains of her old dress had been changed into the most beautiful gown she had ever seen!

Cinderella gasped. A few minutes before, she had been sure she would never attend the ball—never wear a lovely gown, or dance with a handsome partner, or feel joy and excitement in her heart. Now all her dreams were coming true!

"Oh, thank you!" she told her Fairy Godmother as she climbed into the coach. "It's so much more than I had ever hoped for!"

Going Places

from *Dumbo*

A good friend always believes in you.

umbo was the saddest and loneliest little elephant in the circus. First, his mother had been taken away and locked up. And now all the other elephants at the circus would have nothing to do with him. They looked down their trunks at Dumbo's large ears and decided he was a disgrace to elephants everywhere.

Luckily for Dumbo, there was someone besides his mother who thought his ears were beautiful. It was his new friend, little Timothy Mouse.

"Ya know," Timothy said to Dumbo, "lots of people with big ears are famous!" Dumbo's face brightened a bit as Timothy went on. "All we gotta do is build an act! Make you a star! A headliner! Dumbo the Great!"

The only problem was, Timothy wasn't quite sure what it was that Dumbo would be great at. Then they overheard the Ringmaster talking about an idea for a new circus act: a towering pyramid of elephants. That's when the idea came to Timothy. Dumbo could jump from a springboard and land atop the elephant pyramid, waving a flag for a glorious finish!

That night, Timothy whispered the idea into the Ringmaster's ear as he slept. Before Dumbo knew it, he and Timothy were looking on from backstage as the Ringmaster announced the act before a full audience under the big top.

"I give you . . . Dumbo!" proclaimed the Ringmaster.

The elephant pyramid teetered as Dumbo ran full speed across the ring and onto the springboard. But he tripped over his ears and fell flat on his face. He then bounced off the end of the springboard and flew out of control through the air, toppling the tower of elephants. When it was all over, the elephants were bumped, bruised, and cranky. The circus tent was in ruins.

After that, the Ringmaster cast Dumbo as the baby in a ridiculous clown act. The audience loved the silly act, but Dumbo was humiliated.

Timothy tried to cheer him up. "Listen, little fellow," he said, "we may have had a lot of hard luck up till now. But you and me is gonna do big things together!"

Timothy still didn't have a definite plan for Dumbo . . . until early one morning, after Dumbo had dreamed a very vivid dream about flying elephants, and he and Timothy awoke to find themselves sitting on a high branch of a very tall tree. *In a tree?* How had they gotten there? Elephants couldn't climb trees. Dumbo couldn't have jumped up, could he?

Then, Dumbo lost his balance. Timothy and Dumbo fell to the ground below.

"Dumbo!" Timothy exclaimed, putting two and two together. "You flew!" He grabbed Dumbo's ears. "Your ears! Just look at 'em, Dumbo! Why, they're perfect wings! The very things that held you down are now going to carry you up and up and up!" Timothy was practically jumping up and down with excitement. "I can see it all now! Dumbo, the ninth wonder of the universe! The world's only flying elephant!"

It sounded impossible—ridiculous, really.

And yet, Timothy had absolutely no doubt in his friend's ability, which made Dumbo wonder . . . if it just might happen.

Catching the Christmas Spirit

from *Beauty and the Beast: The Enchanted Christmas*

Another person's faith in you can inspire faith in yourself.

All Belle wanted was to find a nice Christmas tree for the Beast. The enchanted pipe organ, Forte, had mentioned that the tree had always been the Master's favorite part of Christmas. So, on Christmas Eve, Belle disregarded her promise never to leave the castle grounds. She took Chip, the teacup, in the horse-drawn sleigh and ventured into the Black Forest to look for the perfect tree—a Christmas tree that would bring some warm, holiday spirit back to the castle.

Unfortunately, the outing went awry, and Chip wound up in the icy river. Belle managed to save him, but Belle herself was still in danger . . . until the Beast appeared and pulled her from the freezing-cold water.

Back at the castle, the angry Beast took Belle straight to the dungeon. "You said you'd never leave!" he yelled.

"I wasn't trying to leave," Belle replied. "I just wanted to make you happy."

But the Beast's growing anger blinded him to the truth. "You broke your word," he said with a growl. "And for that, you'll rot in this dungeon forever!" He stormed out, slamming the iron door behind him.

Later that night, the Beast sat slumped in a chair in the organ chamber as the midnight bells began to ring. It was officially Christmas Day, but there was no joy or festivity in the castle. The Beast had hoped that maybe, just maybe, Belle was the one who could break the spell over him—the one who would love him just as he was. Now that hope seemed lost.

Then the Beast saw a present with his name on it, sitting on the table. It was marked DO NOT OPEN UNTIL CHRISTMAS. "A Christmas present," growled the Beast. "I said no to Christmas." But the Beast decided to open it anyway. He tore open the wrapping paper to find a storybook and a card.

"It's from . . . Belle!" he said in amazement. He realized she must
have left it there the day before. The Beast opened the book, sat
down, and began to read:

"*Once upon a time, there was an enchanted castle. This castle's master
seemed as cold as winter. But deep inside his heart . . .*" The Beast
immediately became engrossed in the story—perhaps because one
of the characters seemed strangely familiar.

He sat reading, his brow furrowed, until he reached the very
last page. Then he smiled as he read the happy ending of the
Christmas tale:

"*That night, the master sang carols and wished upon the Yule log, laughing and sharing the warmth of his friends . . . and loved ones. The End."*

Closing the book, the Beast said to himself, "There is still hope for me." It was surprising that Belle had given him a gift at all. But this gift . . . surely, it was a sign that Belle felt he had a good heart . . . if only he would allow it to warm a bit.

Then the Beast headed for the dungeon, where he found Chip, Mrs. Potts, the teapot, Lumiere, the candelabrum, and Cogsworth, the mantel clock, keeping Belle company. Together they were singing and celebrating the holiday in their own small way. Sheepishly, the Beast joined them.

"Uh, Belle," he said quietly, "can you forgive me?"

Belle smiled at him. "Of course," she replied. "Merry Christmas."

Have Faith, Penny!

from *The Rescuers*

Find faith and you will find a way.

Bianca and Bernard scurried up the steps of the Morningside Orphanage. They had gotten word that an orphan named Penny was in trouble. And Bianca and Bernard were determined to help her.

They soon met Rufus, a cat! But Rufus was too old to chase mice. He preferred to talk to Bernard and Bianca. When asked if he knew Penny, Rufus nodded sadly. The last time he had seen her, Penny was worried that she would never be adopted.

"I told her, 'You've got to believe . . . keep the faith, sweetheart,'" said Rufus. "'Faith is like a bluebird you see from afar. It's for real and as sure as the first evening star. You can't touch it or buy it or wrap it up tight, but it's there just the same, making things turn out right.'"

Rufus told the mice that Penny repeated his words, and seemed to take comfort in them.

"But the next thing I heard," he continued, "Penny was gone."

Bianca and Bernard asked him if he had any idea what could have happened to her. Rufus shook his head, but said he had noticed some funny business with Medusa, a woman who ran a pawnshop down the street. Bianca and Bernard decided to go there next to investigate.

They dashed over to the pawnshop, where they quickly discovered that Medusa had kidnapped Penny. She had taken her away to Devil's

Bayou and was forcing her to search for lost treasure.

It wasn't easy, but Bianca and Bernard made their way to Devil's Bayou, and then to Medusa's riverboat. They found Penny crying in her bedroom. The poor little girl felt hopeless. She didn't know how she would ever get away from Medusa.

Bianca tapped on Penny's hand. "Penny, dear, don't cry. We are here to help you," she said softly.

Penny looked up in surprise at the two mice. She wiped away her tears.

"Didn't you bring anyone big with you? Like the police?" Penny asked her tiny new friends.

"Ah, no . . . there's just the two of us," Bernard confessed.

"But if the three of us work together," Bianca said, "and we have a little faith—"

"Then things will turn out all right!" Penny said, sitting up. Upon remembering Rufus' words, Penny felt better. The three immediately began planning her escape. Bianca and Bernard were not the rescuers she had imagined, but Penny had faith. They could do it. She just knew they could.

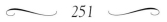

Jane's Change

from *Peter Pan in Return to Never Land*

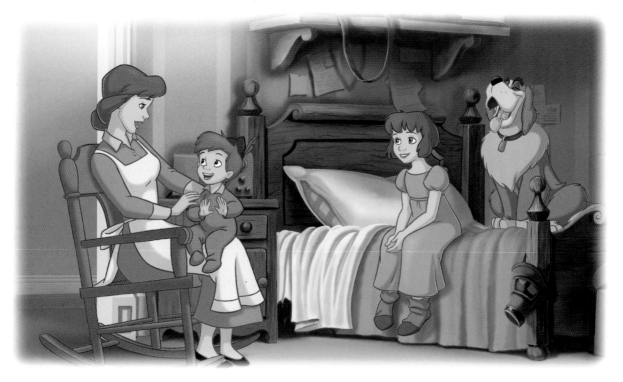

Never stop believing—no matter what.

A long time ago, a young girl named Wendy went on an amazing adventure to a place called Never Land. There she met some wonderful friends whom she would never forget and would always believe in—Peter Pan and the Lost Boys. As the years went by, Wendy got married and had two children, Jane and Danny. She always remembered her friends in Never Land and told her children wonderful stories about her adventures with Peter Pan and the Lost Boys. Jane loved the stories her mother told and hoped to go to Never Land one day, too.

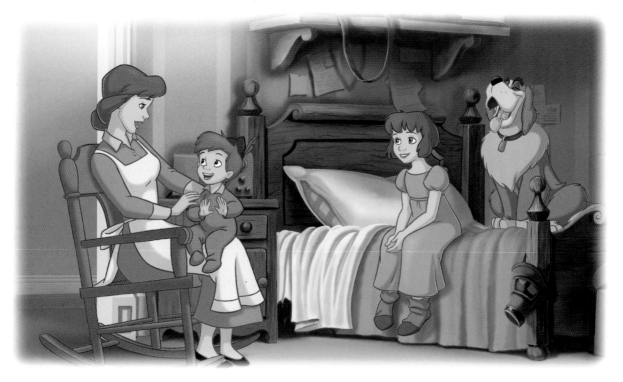

All too soon, a war broke out, and Jane's father had to go off to the army. "I need you to take care of your mom and Danny," her father said gently to her as he left. And though she was still a little girl, Jane took her father's words to heart.

Soon after her father left, Jane stopped believing in Peter Pan and Never Land. She was too grown-up to believe in such things. One day during an air raid, Wendy was trying to convince Danny that the sounds of the planes and bombs were cannons on Captain Hook's ship. Danny danced around the room with his Peter Pan hat and dagger. To help out, Jane gave Danny his birthday gift.

"Happy birthday, Daniel," Jane said. But when Danny opened his gift, all he found were boring old socks. Quickly trying to make the best of the situation, Wendy pretended the socks were puppets and began telling a Peter Pan story. Danny became so excited with the story that he bounced off the bed right into Jane, who was writing in her notebook. "I have no time for your fun and games," Jane said.

"You used to," Danny said. "You were gonna be the first Lost Girl ever!"

Later that evening, Wendy told Jane that she and her brother had to leave the city because it wasn't safe.

"Promise you'll watch over Danny whatever might happen," Wendy said.

"I'm not going!" Jane cried. "I'm staying here."

"Oh, Jane," said Wendy. "We'll be together again. You must have faith."

"Faith, trust, pixie dust. They don't mean anything!" Jane yelled at her mother in frustration. "Peter Pan isn't real and people don't fly. It's just a lot of childish nonsense!"

Jane slammed the door to her bedroom. She was sick of her mother's stories about Never Land. She was a big girl now, too grown-up to believe in kid stuff.

Still pouting, Jane climbed into bed. But shortly after falling asleep, she awoke to a surprise. Captain Hook was in her bedroom! Before she could scream, he stuffed her into a sack and took her back to Never Land in his ship.

Hook was about to throw Jane overboard, but Peter Pan and Tinker Bell rescued her in the nick of time. Then they whisked her away to the Lost Boys' hideout. Jane couldn't believe it. Was she dreaming or did Peter Pan and the Lost Boys really exist? Jane was beginning to think that maybe she shouldn't have stopped believing.

Second Chances

from *102 Dalmatians*

———⊗⊗⊗———

Trust what you know in your heart.

Chloe Simon lived in London with her Dalmatians, Dipstick and Dottie. One day, Dottie had three beautiful puppies. Chloe was as happy as she'd ever been—until she picked up a newspaper and spotted the headline. She gasped in horror. Cruella De Vil had been released from prison!

"You remember her, don't you?" she said, hugging Dipstick. "When I think of what she would have done to you . . ."

Years earlier, Cruella had dognapped all the Dalmatians she could find. She'd wanted to make a fur coat out of them. Luckily, she was stopped and thrown in jail.

Now Cruella was free. The courts trusted that she'd reformed. But Chloe would never trust her. Never!

Cruella immediately took over the Second Chance Dog Shelter. The manager, Kevin, was pleased with his new partner.

"I don't trust anyone who knowingly puts Cruella De Vil near dogs," Chloe told him.

"But she's changed," Kevin replied. "That's why I started Second Chance. I know what it's like to need one."

Chloe still didn't trust Cruella—or Kevin. Not until the day Kevin rescued one of her puppies, Oddball, from floating away on some balloons.

"I don't know how to thank you," she told him, hugging Oddball.

When Kevin invited her to dinner, she agreed. Maybe she *could* trust him—even if he *did* believe in Cruella.

Chloe and Kevin had a wonderful dinner. He told her about his past, and also explained that Cruella had promised to give all her money to the shelter if she ever stole another puppy.

The next day the police discovered several stolen puppies at the shelter. Chloe was shocked. Was Kevin trying to frame Cruella to get her money? The police certainly thought so.

Chloe was heartbroken. She had trusted Kevin and mistrusted Cruella. Now it seemed it should have been the other way around. When Cruella invited Chloe to a dinner party, Chloe accepted.

But Cruella had more than dinner in mind. She locked Chloe in a secret room in her mansion. Cruella still wanted a Dalmatian coat. And she planned to use Chloe's dogs to make it!

Chloe was horrified. Too late, she realized it had been Cruella who had framed Kevin for the puppynapping.

"What a fool I've been!" she murmured. Her heart had been telling her all along to trust Kevin and not Cruella. But she hadn't listened.

In jail, Kevin heard about Cruella's plan. His dogs helped him escape. Meanwhile, at the mansion, Chloe was able to get away as well.

The two met at Chloe's apartment. "Kevin, I'm so sorry," Chloe blurted out. "I should have trusted you—"

"No!" Kevin interrupted. "I should never have trusted Cruella."

Chloe hugged him. Then the two of them worked as a team to find Cruella and the Dalmatians, and together they helped rescue the dogs. Finally, Cruella was sent back to jail and had to donate all her money to Second Chance.

Once again, Chloe was as happy as ever. Her beloved dogs were safe and sound. Plus she had found a special friend that her heart told her she would trust forever.

Journeys to Success

Stories About Teamwork and Determination

The Top Scarer

from *Monsters, Inc.*

———— ❈ ————

Hard work leads to success.

James P. Sullivan, better known as Sulley, loved his job as a Scarer. He took his work seriously. He kept in shape by working out every day, with the encouragement of his best friend, Mike.

"That's it, buddy!" Mike said as Sulley did push-ups. "Work it! Work it! You are number one because you get the job done!"

"*Grrrrr!*" Sulley growled enthusiastically.

Because of the effort he put into his job, Sulley was known as the top Scarer at Monsters, Inc., the factory that processed children's screams into power for the city. The company even featured him in

its TV commercials, showing Sulley doing the famous "Jump 'n' Growl" scare. Soon everyone in Monstropolis knew who he was. When he walked down the street, the other monsters couldn't wait to greet him and wish him well.

Tony the grocer waved as Sulley and Mike walked past on their way to work. "Hey, fellas!" said Tony. "Sulley, I hear you're close to breaking the all-time scare record!"

"Just trying to make sure there're enough screams to go around," Sulley replied modestly.

"Good luck today," Mrs. Tannenbaum said when she saw Sulley. "The whole neighborhood's behind you!"

"We'll do our best!" Sulley promised as he walked on.

Even at work, monsters paid extra attention when Sulley walked by.

"It's the Sullster!" one employee cried.

"How are you doing, big guy?" someone else asked.

"Go get 'em, Mr. Sullivan!" another called.

Sulley had a smile and a kind word for each of his fans. He didn't mind having the other monsters look up to him. He hoped they would see that he really wasn't doing anything they couldn't do if they put their minds to it—it was hard work and dedication that had brought him to the top. It was really quite simple. He loved his job and he worked hard every day. That was what made him the best.

The Surprise

from *Cinderella*

Working together to make someone happy doesn't feel like work at all.

Cinderella could not believe her good fortune. Her stepmother had said that she could go to the royal ball—*if* she finished all of her chores, and *if* she found something suitable to wear.

"I'm sure I can," Cinderella replied. "Oh, thank you, Stepmother." Cinderella tried to contain her excitement as she ran up to her room in the old tower and pulled a dress out of her trunk.

"Isn't it lovely?" she said to her friends, the mice. "It was my mother's." Cinderella draped the dress over a dressmaker's form, then stepped back to take a good look at it. "Well, maybe it is a little old-fashioned. But I'll fix that."

As the mice listened, Cinderella outlined her plans to shorten the sleeves, add a sash and some ruffles, and fix the neckline. But before she could begin work on the dress, Cinderella heard her stepmother and her stepsisters, Anastasia

and Drizella, calling for her. They had more work for her to do.

"Oh, well," Cinderella said with a sigh. "Guess my dress will just have to wait." She headed down the tower stairs as the calls grew louder and more impatient.

Cinderella's little mice friends sadly looked after Cinderella as she left the room. They were worried that her stepmother and her stepsisters would keep her so busy, she wouldn't be ready in time for the ball.

"Work, work, work," Jaq said. "She'll never get her dress done."

"Poor Cinderelly," said little Gus with a sob.

But another little mouse had a big idea. "Hey! We can do it!" she cried. It wouldn't be so hard: if the mice worked together, they could fix Cinderella's dress . . . and surprise her!

They all got right to work. Jaq and Gus sneaked downstairs to search for ribbons and beads to decorate Cinderella's dress, while the rest of the mice began measuring, sewing, cutting, and pinning.

Cinderella's friends, the birds, joined in the effort, too. Each little step was a big task for the tiny creatures. But what they lacked in size, they made up for in number. Everyone wanted to help make a beautiful dress for their friend Cinderella. They could hardly wait to see the look on her face!

The hours flew by. That evening, as the clock struck eight, a carriage pulled up outside the house, ready to carry the ladies to the ball. Sadly, just as Jaq had predicted, Cinderella was not ready. All day long, she had tended to chore after chore. She had not had one free moment to work on her dress.

"I'm not going," Cinderella told her stepmother.

"Not going? Oh, what a shame," her stepmother replied, shooting a wicked smile to Anastasia and Drizella.

Imagine Cinderella's disappointment as she climbed the tower stairs to her room, thinking she would miss out on all the fun. . . .

And imagine her delight when she laid eyes on her dress, completely redesigned by her little friends. It was absolutely beautiful!

"Surprise! Surprise! Surprise!" the mice cried out together.

Cinderella hugged the dress. She didn't know what to say. "Well, I never dreamed it. It's such a surprise. Oh, thank you so much!"

Cinderella's friends knew their hard work had paid off. They had made Cinderella very happy.

Saviors in the Swamp

from *The Rescuers*

If you work together, there is nothing you can't do.

Bernard went to the window of the riverboat and called out to Evinrude the dragonfly. Bernard and his partner, Bianca, had a plan to save Penny, an orphan who had been kidnapped, but they couldn't do it alone.

Bernard told Evinrude to get Elle Mae the beaver and the other animals in the swamp to help them. Evinrude nodded and flew off to the swamp.

The swamp critters already knew about poor Penny's plight. A nasty woman named Medusa and her sidekick Snoops had kidnapped the little girl. They had dragged Penny off into the swamp and forced her to find the priceless Devil's Eye diamond. Luckily for Penny, all of her new little friends were working together to plot her escape.

The swamp animals had been anxiously awaiting Bernard and Bianca's signal.

At last, Evinrude arrived and gasped out the order.

"Charge!" they all cried, and raced to the riverboat.

In the meantime, Medusa was holding Penny and Snoops at gunpoint. Now that she had the

diamond—which was hidden in Penny's teddy bear—she wasn't going to share the riches with Snoops as the two had planned. And she was going to abandon Penny in the swamp.

"If either of you tries to follow me, you'll get blasted," Medusa threatened as she backed her way toward the door.

But Bernard and Bianca were ready. They quickly stretched a wire across her path.

Medusa tripped and fell on her back. Her gun fired in the air, and the teddy bear flew out of her hands. "My diamond!" she cried.

Snoops and Penny both rushed forward, but Penny was faster. She grabbed the bear just as the swamp folk arrived. The animals saw Medusa on the ground and let her have it.

Medusa's helpers, two wicked crocodiles, were close at hand. Fortunately, Bianca and Bernard had a plan for the crocodiles, too. Bianca squirted some of her perfume into the boat's old iron elevator. Then one of their swamp friends dangled the mice on a fishhook in front of the elevator. The crocodiles smelled

the perfume, saw the mice, and ran right into the trap! "Now!" cried Bernard. The door to the elevator slammed shut.

Penny and the animals dashed out of the riverboat. Earlier, their rabbit friend had found a bunch of fireworks. Snoops used to set them off to signal Medusa when she was out in the swamp. As everyone clambered onto Medusa's swamp mobile, they shot fireworks at the riverboat. They shot so many that the riverboat exploded!

Before they could get away, Medusa managed to grab a rope hanging down from the swamp mobile. The explosion freed the crocodiles, and now she was riding their backs like water skis! Penny turned the steering wheel quickly, the rope jerked, and Medusa went flying back to the sinking riverboat. The swamp mobile sped away.

Penny and the animals looked back and cheered. The plan had worked perfectly. They had all worked together, and now Penny was free.

Eeyore's Hard Luck

from *The Tigger Movie*

Good friends work together when things get rocky.

One day, Tigger was out and about in the Hundred-Acre Wood, looking for someone to bounce with him. He had already asked his friends, Winnie the Pooh, Piglet, and Kanga, but they were all too busy. Tigger sat himself down on a big boulder. It looked like he would be bouncing all by himself. But soon he felt more hopeful. "There're plenty of others I haven't asked yet!" he reminded himself. And with that, Tigger bounced off the boulder and went on his way.

Tigger didn't know it, but as he sprang up from the boulder, it came loose and started to roll down a cliff. It was going faster and

faster, and it was headed straight for Eeyore's house! Eeyore heard

some pebbles hit his roof, so he stepped outside to take a look— just in time to see the boulder flatten his home.

Poor Eeyore. What was he going to do? He couldn't move a big boulder like that all by himself. He was very sad, indeed.

When Eeyore's friends heard what had happened, they came right away.

"Are you all right?" asked Piglet.

"Wow. Look at the size of it," said Roo, shaking his head.

Pooh, Piglet, and the others wanted to help Eeyore, but they didn't know what to do. Rabbit, naturally, took charge of the situation.

"Your attention, please. I have officially completed the plans," he announced.

"What plans?" asked Pooh.

"*The* plans," Rabbit explained, "for removing this boulder and restoring Eeyore to his happy home. All we need is a little team effort."

And so the group set to work on "Rabbit's Rock Remover." Within a short while, a rather complicated tangle of wheels, pulleys, and ropes was attached to the boulder. Everything was ready.

"Pooh Bear! Release the counterweight! Kanga and Roo, start depressurizing the granite extractor!" Rabbit directed. The wheels started spinning, the pulleys started pulling, and the ropes started roping . . . but the boulder wouldn't budge.

"Perhaps we could use another helping hand," suggested Kanga. She knew that if all the friends in the Hundred-Acre Wood came together, then surely they would find a way to move the boulder.

At that very moment, Tigger bounded in. He was still searching for a bouncing partner. Rabbit was in no mood. "Look! Just look at all the work we have to do!" Rabbit scolded as he pointed out the boulder to Tigger.

But Tigger was just the helper the group needed. He took one look at the rock and said, "What? Movin' that old thing? Not a problem. All you need is a little bouncin'."

Tigger wound up, soared through the air, and landed on just the right spot.

The boulder budged! In fact, it began rolling through the woods. Pooh and his friends got caught up in "Rabbit's Rock Remover" and were pulled along with it. With a thump, they landed in the creek. They were wet and dirty, but it was worth it—they had helped their friend Eeyore.

The Ants' Only Chance

from *A Bug's Life*

The only failure is the failure to try.

ot quickly hid behind some grass as two big grasshoppers walked by. They were talking about their leader's plans for the ant colony. One explained to the other, "After we get the food, he'll squish the Queen to show who's boss. She's dead; they cry, 'boohoo'; we go home; end of story."

Dot gasped. The ants needed help! She knew that the only one who could save them was her friend Flik. But the colony had banished him.

All Flik had ever wanted to do was make life easier for the ants. He invented all kinds of new gadgets. But lately, his ideas had gotten the colony into big trouble. First, his grain-picking machine had destroyed the ants' food offering to the grasshoppers. Then, when he went to find warriors to fight the grasshoppers, he accidentally brought back circus performers instead. The colony was so fed up with Flik that they sent him and his circus bugs away.

But Dot was sure that Flik's latest invention was the colony's only chance. Before Flik had been banished, he had built a huge fake bird to scare the grasshoppers away. It was brilliant! But without Flik at the controls, the other ants would never be able to fly it.

Dot raced to find Flik and the circus bugs. When she found them, she quickly explained the situation.

"We have to do something!" cried Rosie the spider.

"I know!" said Manny the praying mantis. "The bird!"

But then, to everyone's surprise, Flik shook his head and said, "The bird won't work. The colony is right. I just make things worse. That bird is a guaranteed failure. Just like me."

Flik used to believe in himself and his inventions, but his confidence was shaken. His friends tried to boost Flik's spirits and encourage him to give the mechanical bird a try.

"We'll follow you into battle," Francis the ladybug told him.

"We believe in you," said Manny.

But still, Flik was afraid that his invention wouldn't work. He just couldn't risk failing again.

Then Dot handed Flik a little rock. "Pretend it's a seed, okay?" she asked him.

A few days earlier, Dot had complained to Flik about being too little to fly. Flik had assured her that being small wasn't so bad. He had held up a rock and asked her to pretend it was a seed. "Everything that made that giant tree is already contained in this tiny little seed," he told her.

Flik looked down at the rock and smiled. "Thanks, Dot," he said.

Even though defeating the grasshoppers seemed like an impossible task, he knew he had to try. "All right," Flik said with resolve. "Let's do it!"

"That's the Flik we all know and love!" said Gypsy the moth, as they hurried to prepare the bird for flight.

With Flik's determination back, surely there was nothing the ant colony could not accomplish!

Down but Not Out

from *The Great Mouse Detective*

Don't take yourself out of the game.

asil and Dawson had walked right into the evil Ratigan's trap. Thinking that they were hot on the villain's trail, the renowned detective and the gentlemanly doctor had followed Ratigan's peg-legged bat, Fidget, through the sewers under London. They watched from the shadows as Fidget darted into a wine barrel.

"Dawson, we've found it!" Basil whispered. "Ratigan's secret lair!"

But Ratigan and his men were waiting for them. A bright light came on as a banner reading WELCOME, BASIL! was unfurled, and Ratigan's men jumped out and cried, "Surprise!"

Ratigan cackled in wicked delight. "You fool," he said with a sneer. "Isn't it clear to you yet? The superior mind has triumphed! I've won!"

Within minutes, Ratigan's men had tied Basil and Dawson to a specially rigged mousetrap. The trap was hooked up to an old-fashioned phonograph playing a tune, and to a gun, a crossbow, and an ax—

all pointed straight at Basil and Dawson. When the song was over, the trap would be sprung and . . .

"*Snap! Boom! Twang! Thunk! Splat!*" said Ratigan. "And so ends the short, undistinguished career of Basil of Baker Street." Finally, Ratigan left them to their fate while he and his men headed to Buckingham Palace to complete his dastardly scheme. He was going to replace Queen Moustoria with a robot queen under his control!

Once Ratigan was gone, Basil began to blame himself. "Ratigan's proved he's more clever than I. He would never have walked into such an obvious trap."

Dawson eyed the phonograph nervously as the song played on. "Pull yourself together!" he said, trying to encourage Basil. "You can stop that villain!"

But Basil just stared blankly off into space.

"Dash it all!" Dawson exclaimed. "We're about to be horribly *splatted* and all you can do is lie there, feeling sorry for yourself?" This was not at all the Basil whom Dawson respected and admired. "Well, I know you can save us, but if you've given up, then why don't we just set it off now and be done with it?"

Seemingly hurt by Dawson's sarcastic words, Basil turned his head away and slowly, sadly closed his eyes. Then suddenly, his eyes popped open and he raised his eyebrows in a curious expression.

"Set it off now . . . ? Set it . . . off . . . now?" Basil muttered, formulating a plan in his mind. "Yes! We'll set the trap off *now*!"

Dawson was horrified. He hadn't been serious. But Basil had an escape plan. Quick as lightning, Basil's eyes skimmed over every inch of the trap. He figured out that if he and Dawson tripped the trap early, one of the mechanisms would jam, and the trap would be foiled!

On Basil's command, they set off a chain reaction exactly as Basil had predicted: the mousetrap jammed, the gun misfired, the crossbow fell over, and the ax handle broke. The ax head did come crashing down on the mousetrap, but it missed Basil and Dawson and sliced the trap into two pieces, cutting through the ropes that tied them down.

They were free and safe, thanks to Basil's quick thinking . . . and Dawson's determination to escape.

Nani Goes It Alone

from *Lilo & Stitch*

Don't let anything keep you from your goals.

ani had taken care of her sister ever since their parents died. It wasn't easy—Lilo could be difficult, and Nani had to work hard to make ends meet.

One day, Nani was late picking up Lilo from hula class. When she arrived, she discovered that Lilo had already left.

"Oh, no!" Nani said as she ran home, hoping that Lilo would be there. Lilo was there, but that wasn't the end of Nani's problems. She still had to deal with a visit from their social worker, Cobra Bubbles.

The house was a mess. Cobra Bubbles frowned as he looked around. "You left the stove on while you were out?" he asked Nani.

Just then, Lilo walked in to the kitchen. Nani introduced her to Cobra Bubbles.

"Let's talk about you," Cobra Bubbles said to Lilo. "Are you happy?"

Lilo tried to give him the right answers. But she got a little confused. Cobra Bubbles was concerned.

"In case you're wondering," he told Nani as he left, "this didn't go well."

Nani had to make Cobra Bubbles see that Lilo belonged with her. But how?

Nani decided they should get a pet. Maybe if Lilo were less lonely, she would be happier—maybe Cobra Bubbles would like that! She let Lilo pick out a dog at the animal shelter.

At first, that only made things worse. The dog, Stitch, looked strange and behaved very badly. He even got Nani fired from her job!

Now Nani was really in trouble. If she didn't find a new job soon, Cobra Bubbles would take Lilo away! But it wasn't easy finding a job when she had to spend all her time trying to keep Lilo and Stitch out of trouble.

Just when Nani was ready to give up, her friend David brought good news. He had found a job for her!

Nani rushed off, making Lilo promise to stay home. But a pair of aliens appeared while she was away, and tried to capture Stitch. They wrecked Lilo's house.

That was the last straw. Cobra Bubbles put Lilo in his car.

"You know I have no choice," he told Nani.

As Nani and Cobra Bubbles argued, Lilo slipped out of the car.

Nani chased her, but discovered that an alien had taken Lilo onto his ship!

Nani was sure this was the end of their little family. Then Stitch appeared. He wanted to help save Lilo!

That gave Nani new strength. With the help of Stitch, David, and even some good aliens, Nani got Lilo back.

Cobra Bubbles was impressed. He agreed that Nani took good care of Lilo, despite the earlier problems. They could stay together!

Nani would still have to work hard to make ends meet. But now that she had faced the worst, she was ready to hope for the best.

Dogs Can Fly!

from *102 Dalmatians*

If you believe in yourself, you might find yourself soaring to new heights.

Waddlesworth was a macaw who thought he was a dog. He lived at the Second Chance Dog Shelter.

"Fight night!" he crowed as the shelter's manager, Kevin, played tug-of-war with several dogs.

But the dogs were playing a trick on Kevin and rolled him into a cage. "Hey, that's not fair!" he cried.

Soon it was dinnertime. Waddlesworth grabbed his bowl in his beak and barked for food. Kevin put some food in a birdhouse. "Hop up to your house," he cried. "Come on, Waddlesworth! Fly!"

"Dogs can't fly!" Waddlesworth grumbled.

The next day, Kevin took the whole gang to a puppet show. "One adult, three dogs, and one bird," he told the ticket seller.

Waddlesworth let out a sharp bark.

"Four dogs, please," Kevin corrected himself.

Just then, Kevin's new friend, Chloe, showed up with her Dalmatians. Kevin introduced all the dogs to one another.

One of the Dalmatian puppies, Oddball, stared at Waddlesworth. Then she barked at him. Waddlesworth barked back.

During the show, Oddball got tangled in some balloon strings.

"Oh, no!" Chloe cried as the puppy floated up out of reach.

"Waddlesworth!" Kevin exclaimed. "You can save that puppy. All you have to do is fly up there. Fly!"

Waddlesworth hopped off Kevin's shoulder. Instead of soaring up, he plummeted straight down.

He shook his head. "Dogs can't fly!"

Luckily, Kevin managed to save Oddball. But soon a new problem arose—Cruella De Vil was back and was up to her old tricks. Her henchman snatched Oddball's family right out of Chloe's apartment.

Waddlesworth arrived at the train station with Kevin and Chloe. They had figured out that Cruella was taking the Dalmatians to Paris. They heard barking and saw that Oddball had escaped from Cruella. She was trotting beside the train, trying to figure out how to save her family.

"Don't jump!" Waddlesworth cried. If Oddball tried to vault onto the train, she would be hurt!

Waddlesworth leaped off Kevin's head. Suddenly, he was gliding through the air! He gulped as he realized what he had done.

"Flap your wings!" Kevin shouted. "You can do it! You're a bird!"

"Flap wings?" Waddlesworth murmured. Noticing that he was losing altitude, he flapped— and rose back into the air! "Flap wings!" he cried happily. "Dogs can flyyyyy!"

He swooped down and grabbed Oddball by the scruff of the neck, flying right onto the train with her. Thanks to the

flying dog, Oddball had a chance to save her family!

Waddlesworth and Oddball rode the train all the way to Paris. Once they arrived, Waddlesworth helped Oddball track down Cruella and rescue the other Dalmatians. Waddlesworth was proud of himself for helping the puppies. He was even prouder to be the only dog in London that could fly!

Saving the Sultan

from *Aladdin: The Return of Jafar*

Friends and family are always worth fighting for.

Aladdin could hardly believe how well things were going for him. Ever since he and his friends had defeated the Sultan's evil vizier, Jafar, Agrabah had been very peaceful.

One evening, the Sultan invited Aladdin to a special dinner.

"Aladdin, you have proved to be a man of strong moral character," he said. "I've decided to make you my new royal vizier!"

Aladdin was thrilled. Accepting the honor, he vowed to do his best.

It wasn't long before his vow was put to the test. Jafar had returned, and he had wicked plans for the Sultan. . . .

Aladdin and the Sultan were enjoying a quiet day near the river when a gang of mysterious masked men appeared. The men were riding huge, frightening, winged horses, and they grabbed the Sultan before Aladdin could stop them.

"Aladdin!" the Sultan cried in terror.

"Come on, Carpet!" Aladdin cried, jumping on the Magic Carpet and speeding after them.

He caught up to them in front of a waterfall. Swooping down, Aladdin grabbed the Sultan away from his captors.

"Hang on, Sultan!" he cried as the carpet raced to the top of the waterfall. "This is where we lose them!"

But one winged horse followed. Suddenly, a magical whirlpool appeared in the water below and sucked in the Sultan. He cried out in fear as he was swirled around and around in the churning water.

"We have to go back, Carpet!" Aladdin cried.

The Magic Carpet sped back, and Aladdin tried to save the Sultan from the whirlpool. Instead, he got sucked into the water himself!

He fought the current, but it was too strong for him. Before he knew what was happening, he had been swept far downstream.

The mysterious captors escaped with the Sultan. Aladdin managed to crawl to shore, coughing and sputtering. But he wasn't ready to give up. Far from it! The Sultan was counting on Aladdin—his vizier, his trusted friend—and Aladdin was never going to give up until the Sultan was safe.

Roo's Big Bounce

from *The Tigger Movie*

A lot of practice can help you succeed.

Roo looked up to Tigger as if Tigger were Roo's big brother. Whatever Tigger did, Roo wanted to do, too—especially when it came to bouncing.

One afternoon when Roo and Tigger were outside bouncing together, Tigger mentioned the Whoop-de-Dooper Loop-de-Looper Alley-Ooper Bounce. "It's the most hardest bounce only the bestest bouncer can bounce," Tigger told Roo.

"I could bounce it," said Roo.

"What? That's ridickerous!" replied Tigger. "It's a very powerful

bounce! And it's only for professional bouncers."

Roo just knew he could learn the Whoop-de-Dooper Loop-de-Looper Alley-Ooper Bounce. He pleaded with Tigger to teach him.

"You swing yer legs up high," Tigger said, "and twist yer tail in tight . . . wind up all yer springs and . . . with your eyes fixated straight ahead . . . let it all loose!"

Roo followed all the steps, but when he let it all loose, he crashed into the closet.

That night, before he went to bed, Roo practiced the Whoop-de-Dooper Loop-de-Looper Alley-Ooper Bounce. He twisted and tucked and concentrated with all his might. This time, when he let it all loose, he crashed first into the toy chest, then into his mother, Kanga.

Roo wanted to learn the bounce for himself, but he also wanted to learn it for Tigger. Tigger didn't like being the only expert bouncer—and lone tigger—in the Hundred-Acre Wood. He wanted to be part of a whole family of tiggers.

"Maybe, if I do it really good for Tigger, he wouldn't miss having a family so much," Roo told Kanga.

Roo wasn't the only one who was trying to cheer up Tigger.

All of Tigger's friends were working hard at it too. It seemed, though, as if nothing would work. A sad and lonely Tigger went off into the woods by himself and was gone for quite some time. Pooh and the others were worried about Tigger's being out all alone in the cold. They searched high and low until at last they found Tigger, sitting up in a tree. But soon after they got there, a great big rumble came from the mountain above them. Mounds of snow came whooshing down the mountain, headed straight for them!

Tigger quickly bounced down from the tree, grabbed Roo, and nestled him safely on a high branch. Then, in short order, he filled the tree branches with Pooh, Piglet, Eeyore, and Rabbit, too. But the rushing snow caught up with Tigger and swept him up on a rock and out toward a cliff!

Roo gathered up all of his courage. He just knew the Whoop-de-Dooper Loop-de-Looper Alley-Ooper Bounce could save Tigger! So,

Roo twisted himself up and thought about the bounce with even more might than ever before. When he let it all loose, he flew through the air and landed right on Tigger's rock! Roo helped Tigger bounce to safety just in time.

Roo had saved the day! All his practice had paid off just when his friend needed him the most. And he had done the Whoop-de-Dooper Loop-de-Looper Alley-Ooper Bounce as well as any tigger ever could.

Pulling Together

from *Toy Story 2*

Anything is possible when you're part of a good team.

Woody had been toynapped by Al of Al's Toy Barn, and his friends were ready to rush to his rescue. "Woody once risked his life to save me," Buzz Lightyear announced. "I can't call myself his friend if I'm not willing to do the same."

"I'm coming with you," Slinky Dog told Buzz.

Rex the dinosaur, Hamm the pig, and Mr. Potato Head all agreed to help, too.

That night, the toys sneaked out of the house onto the roof. It was a long way down. Luckily, Slinky was there. He helped the others get down safely.

They courageously made their way across town and soon spotted Al's Toy Barn. There was just one problem: it stood on the other side of a wide, busy street.

"There must be a safe way across," Buzz said.

Suddenly, he had an idea. There were some orange traffic cones nearby. Buzz told the others to put them over their heads. Despite causing a traffic jam, they were able to rush safely across the lanes of traffic.

Woody wasn't inside the store, but Al was on the phone. They overheard him say he was selling Woody to a toy museum! The toys just *had* to get to Woody, so they followed Al to his apartment, and climbed up to his floor, helping one another all the way.

There, they watched in horror as Al packed Woody and some other toys into a special carrying case. They ran to the elevator to follow Woody.

But just then, Zurg—Buzz's archenemy—appeared! He had followed them from the toy store. Zurg was very strong—even stronger than Buzz.

But then Rex spun around, accidentally knocking Zurg over with his tail. He tumbled off the roof and disappeared. Rex had saved the day!

Woody still needed saving, though. The friends followed Al outside. He climbed into his car and drove away. "How are we going to get Woody now?" Rex cried.

Mr. Potato Head pointed to a pizza truck parked nearby. "Pizza, anyone?" he said.

The toys hopped into the truck. Buzz climbed toward the steering wheel. "Slink, you take the pedals," he said. "Rex, you navigate. Hamm and Potato, operate the levers and knobs."

The toys did as they were told. The truck started!

As they pulled into the street, the toys were excited. Each of them was doing his part to make the rescue mission work. They made a great team. Nothing could stop them from saving Woody now!

An Unlikely Pair

from *The Emperor's New Groove*

Two backs are stronger than one.

"Kuzco!" cried Pacha. "Quick! Help me up!"

Pacha had been leading the emperor-turned-llama Kuzco through the jungle and back to the city where Kuzco lived. They were crossing an old bridge when, all of a sudden, the bridge collapsed. Pacha fell through! Now he was hanging on for dear life.

"No, I don't think I will," Kuzco said coldly.

Kuzco could see the palace from where he stood, so he saw no reason to help this peasant. Kuzco could find his way back home on his own now.

"Buh-bye," said Kuzco.

He turned to walk away when . . . the bridge gave way beneath him, too! He was dangling by the ropes, just like Pacha.

"Are you okay?" asked a genuinely concerned Pacha.

"Yeah, I think I'm all right," replied the dazed Kuzco.

"Good," said Pacha, as he punched Kuzco square in the jaw.

Of course, Pacha had every reason to be angry, but it really wasn't an ideal time for a fistfight. Still, the two punched and kicked, and soon they both lost hold of the ropes. Down they fell, until they got wedged in a narrow crevice. They were still high above the river.

Hungry alligators snapped and circled in the water below.

There was no more time for arguing.

"Now, we're gonna have to work together to get out of this, so follow my lead," directed Pacha.

Pacha was quite used to teamwork. But Kuzco was used to people working *for* him, not *with* him. But he had no choice. If he didn't learn to cooperate fast, they would both be alligator food. Pacha showed him what to do. The two pushed their backs together, and walked their way up the crevice.

"Look! We're moving!" cried Kuzco, surprised that the plan was actually working.

As they approached the top, the crevice widened.

Pacha saw a rope from the bridge, hanging down nearby. If only he could get to it, they could pull themselves up to the ledge.

"You're gonna have to trust me," Pacha told Kuzco, as he explained his idea.

Kuzco strained his neck and pushed Pacha up toward the rope. He reached it! With a final effort, they got themselves onto the ledge. They lay there for a moment, safe but stunned.

Suddenly, the ledge beneath Pacha began to crumble. Just in the nick of time, Kuzco caught Pacha's shirt in his teeth and pulled him to solid ground.

Luckily for both of them, Kuzco's crash course in teamwork was a success. He was beginning to see that sometimes the only way to work was to work together.

Love Will Find a Way

from *Sleeping Beauty*

True love can overcome all obstacles in its path.

Flora, Fauna, and Merryweather had come to free Prince Phillip from Maleficent's dungeon. Now, the prince could hurry off to King Stefan's castle, where his true love, Princess Aurora, lay in a deep sleep under Maleficent's evil spell. One kiss from the prince and the spell would be broken.

"Wait, Prince Phillip!" cried Flora. "The road to true love may be barred by still many more dangers, which you alone will have to face."

Magically, a shield and a sword appeared in Prince Phillip's hands.

"So, arm thyself with this enchanted Shield of Virtue and this mighty Sword of Truth," Flora continued, "for these weapons of righteousness will triumph over evil."

The prince and the fairies made their way out of the dungeon. Maleficent's henchmen were after them at once. Prince Phillip fought them off while the fairies disappeared out a window. The prince jumped out after them and slid down a pile of debris into the courtyard, where his horse was shackled.

"Phillip, watch out!" Flora called to him.

Maleficent's henchmen were dropping boulders from atop the castle walls, aiming at the prince. Flora used her magic to change the boulders into bubbles. Next, the henchmen shot arrows at the prince, but again Flora protected him, turning the deadly arrows into harmless flowers. Merryweather zapped the chains off the horse's legs, and in a flash, the prince was racing away from Maleficent's castle.

Enraged at Phillip's escape, Maleficent hurled lightning bolts at

him from her tower. Phillip's horse reared as the lightning bolts just missed them, striking the ground and making the way ahead rocky and rough. But the prince rode on.

Maleficent summoned stronger magic. Raising her staff, she cast a spell, and a thicket of thorns sprung up around King Stefan's castle, barring Prince Phillip's path to his beloved Aurora. But still the prince went on, hacking his way through the thorns with his sword.

"No!" Maleficent bellowed, her anger growing ever stronger. "It cannot be!" Then, in a fiery whirlwind of magic and fury, Maleficent transported herself to the base of King Stefan's castle and took the form of an enormous dragon. She stood between the castle and Prince Phillip, shooting out flames.

The prince charged, aiming his sword at the dragon. But the monster knocked him off his horse with one fiery hiss.

"Up! Up this way!" Flora called out to Prince Phillip from nearby. Following the fairies' lead, the prince climbed up the cliff while the flames drew closer and closer. Then, as Phillip slashed at the dragon's head with his sword, his shield was knocked out of his hand. He was left with only his sword to protect himself.

Flora sprinkled the sword with fairy dust, saying, "*Now Sword of Truth, fly swift and sure, that evil die and good endure!*"

Prince Phillip aimed the sword and threw it at the dragon. It flew straight into the dragon's heart, causing the monster to rear back, then plunge forward over the edge of the cliff.

Maleficent was defeated.

Then, Prince Phillip hurried into King Stefan's castle and up to the tower, where he found Aurora lying in a deep sleep. At long last, nothing stood between the prince and his one true love, Princess Aurora. He kissed her. The spell was finally broken, and they lived happily ever after.

Never Give Up

from *Atlantis: The Lost Empire*

Never give up on your dreams.

Milo Thatch had spent his whole life studying dead languages and doing research in dusty old books. That was the only way he knew to fulfill his grandest dream—finding the lost city of Atlantis. One winter, he spent all his spare time huddled over his desk in the basement of the museum where he worked. He was trying to figure out the clues in an obscure old book that described something called *The Shepherd's Journal*, which was supposed to contain a map to Atlantis. Finally, he had a breakthrough.

Milo practiced a speech explaining his discovery. "After comparing the text to the runes on the Viking shield, I found that one of the letters had been mistranslated," he proclaimed to the empty basement. "By changing this letter and inserting the correct one, we find that the key to Atlantis lies not in Ireland, but in Iceland."

He tried to convince the museum board members to listen to his new theory. But they thought Milo was crazy for spending so much time trying to find a place that probably didn't exist at all. They started running away whenever they saw him, just to avoid having to listen to him talk about Atlantis.

But Milo never let their doubts sway him. He was sure that Atlantis was out there somewhere. Would he ever get a chance to prove it?

One day, a wealthy man named Preston Whitmore summoned Milo to his mansion. Milo wasn't sure what the man wanted at first. Then Whitmore pulled out a dusty old book. Milo gasped. It was *The Shepherd's Journal!*

That was just the key Milo needed to figure out how to reach Atlantis. But it wouldn't do him much good on dry land. He needed to find a way to put the map to use.

"I will find Atlantis," he cried excitedly, "if I have to rent a rowboat!"

Whitmore leaned closer. "Congratulations, Milo," he said. "This is exactly what I wanted to hear. But forget the rowboat, son. We'll travel in style!"

Milo gasped as he realized what this meant. Whitmore wanted to fund an expedition to find Atlantis. And he wanted Milo to guide it!

Before he knew it, Milo was standing on the deck of an enormous, state-of-the-art submarine called the *Ulysses*. A full crew was along to help him search for the lost city.

Milo could hardly believe it. After all the dreams, all the studying, all the hard work and disappointments and ridicule, his persistence was paying off at last. He had never given up on his dreams—and now they were about to come true!

A Pecking Problem

from *A Bug's Life*

A single foe is no match for a clever team.

The circus bugs were leaving the anthill. Flik had hired them to help the ants fight the dreaded grasshoppers. He thought they were warriors, but it turned out they were only circus performers. Flik was sure that if the colony found this out, then it would never forgive him for his blunder.

"Please, please, don't go," Flik begged them.

Then Flik glanced over his shoulder. They were standing right in front of a sparrow's nest. And the sparrow was in it!

"Run!" Flik yelled as he took off in the opposite direction.

The circus bugs didn't see the bird. They were confused. First Flik said stay, then he said go . . . what did Flik want from them? But then the bird's shadow fell upon them. The bugs screamed and ran away as fast as they could.

As they scattered, they heard a small voice cry out, "Flik!"

It was Dot, the colony's young ant princess. She couldn't quite fly yet and she was falling from the sky—right into the bird's path.

Francis the ladybug was closest to Dot. "I got you, I got you," he reassured her as he zipped into position beneath her.

He caught her just in time, but he couldn't bear the extra weight. The two fell down together into a crack in the riverbed, and Francis broke one of his legs. Immediately, the sparrow swooped down to the  ground. It pecked and pecked at the crack. Francis and Dot were trapped!

"They're in trouble!" cried Manny the praying mantis.

Flik and the circus bugs had to do something quick to save their friends. They couldn't fight a big bird, twenty times their size, but they could work together to try to outsmart it. It was their only hope!

"Yoo-hoo! Mr. Early Bird!" Heimlich the caterpillar called out. Slim the walking stick was holding him up in the air, trying to distract the sparrow.

The sparrow lifted its head and began hopping toward the juicy caterpillar.

In the meantime, Flik and the other bugs flew above Dot and Francis. Rosie the spider spun a web and lowered it into the crack. The pill bugs helped Francis and Dot get into the net quickly.

But now, Heimlich was in trouble! The sparrow was getting closer. Slim had dropped down into a crack, but Heimlich was stuck. He was too fat.

"Suck it in, man!" cried Slim.

The sparrow was just about to reach the caterpillar, when Gypsy the moth quickly flew in front of it. In the split second the sparrow was distracted, Slim yanked Heimlich down into the hole.

The sparrow finally turned from the crack and saw Dim the rhino beetle flying away, carrying Flik and his friends. The pill bugs saw the bird coming and tried to alert Dim. "Up, up, up, up!" they yelled to him.

Dim flew high in the air and then nose-dived down into some thick thornbushes. The sparrow tried to follow, but the thorns hurt its feet. The bugs looked back with relief and watched the bird fly away.

None of the bugs could have defeated the sparrow alone. But thanks to their quick and clever teamwork, they all were safe.